I0761980

CHARLIE O'BRIEN, PRIVATE INVESTIGATOR

DO NOT MISS ALAN DALE DICKINSON'S PREVIOUSLY PUBLISHED CRIME-FICTION MYSTERIES:

"Charlie O'Brien, Private Investigator"

"Kidnap Country"

"The Money Changer"

"For the Love of Money"

"Charlie's Private Eye Angels"

In addition, a published short primer on:
"How to Write a Novel" (In seven easy steps)

CHARLIE O'BRIEN, PRIVATE INVESTIGATOR

BY PROFESSOR
ALAN DALE DICKINSON

This book is a work of fiction. All of the characters, organizations, companies, and events portrayed in this novel are either products of the author's imagination, or are used fictitiously. Some scenarios that are featured in this tale are creative liberties taken by the author where necessary in the interest of easy readability and faster pacing.

ISBN: 978-1-7326283-1-1

"CHARLIE O'BRIEN, PRIVATE INVESTIGATOR"

DICKINSON PUBLISHING COMPANY

PROFESSOR ALAN DALEDICKINSON
Chairman and Chief Executive Officer

Bank of America
Vice President and Business Banking Manager (Retired)
World Corporate Lending Group
P.O. Box 3962
Laguna Hills, CA 92654

DEDICATION

This book, *Charlie O'Brien, Private Investigator,* is dedicated to my precious granddaughter, Morgan Marie Dickinson. She is the best grandkid in the whole wide world. I hope that the rest of you grandparents out there will understand my admitted favoritism.

ACKNOWLEDGEMENT

This novel, *Charlie O'Brien, Private Investigator,* might never have come to fruition and completion had it not been for the encouragement and friendship of a few very kind-hearted people. At the top of my short list, a special thank you to a long-time friend, Curt.

Also, Leann, John, Lindsay, and Zack, whom all have a lot of love for hurting, sad, and lonely people. There are so many very lonely individuals in the world today. Where do they all come from?
To my eldest son, David Alan, who has a heart made out of silver, and to his wonderful and smart wife, Desiree'. To my younger son, Mark Alan, who has a heart made out of gold, and to his talented bride, Ramona. And to my very precious niece, Jules, and sons Kyle and T.J.

Also, my adopted mother, Betty, and my long-time supporter, Phyllis. And my good friend, Howard, who lets me vent to him about my many 'trials and tribulations' in this crazy old world we find ourselves living in today. And he acted as my very capable research assistant who, without his computer skills and savvy, this book would not have been nearly as interesting nor realistic.

In the final analysis, I would have to say this book is inspired by my lifelong affinity for detective novels, movies, television programs all these many years here on old planet earth.

PROLOGUE

A little information concerning the author...

The author has presented this novel, *Charlie O'Brien, Private Investigator*, with a few ideas in conception, theology, and ideology. To keep this book simple (KISS-keep it simple stupid), easy, fun, and fast to read, as well as, most of all, to bring a little bit of levity and enjoyment into the lives of some people.

These individuals are dealing with the worldwide economic financial crisis, loss of jobs, loss of homes, loss of loved ones, loss of friends and beloved family members, as well as adversaries attacking from every side.

Its concept is based upon, although not completely, a work of fiction, radio shows, movies, television programs, detective novels, newspaper articles, studies, research, historical evidence, an assorted volume of facts, theories, and, of course, the writer's vivid imagination provided helpful insights while writing this book, as well as the writer's lifelong interest in Private Investigators and Private Detectives.

In addition, I have included a little bit of personal insight that I have gleaned from my 35 years in the banking business, teaching, real estate, and security professions And, working very closely with law enforcement agencies and the FBI in and around Los Angeles, California.

I hold a Bachelor of Arts degree from the Mihaylo College of Business and Economics at California State University at Fullerton, with concentrations in the business subject matters of: a) accounting, b) economics, c) finance, d) management, and e) real estate.

In addition, I hold a lifetime teaching credential in business and banking from the State of California Department of Education. This enables the author to teach at any Community College located in the State of California.

And I once held a securities license (stock broker license) for the sale of stocks, bonds, and mutual funds, as well as a State of California insurance license to sell life insurance, retirement plans, and annuities to major corporations, hospitals, and other businesses in California.

And I have received numerous recognitions, awards, and good merit certificates over the past 35 years from many different organizations I have been associated/employed with, way too many to list here.

I am sorry to say that I did not yet complete my Masters of Business Administration (MBA) in International Business Banking and World Economics, unfortunately.

However, I was accepted and enrolled in this very prestigious graduate program at Cal State University, Fullerton. Due to many stresses in my life at that time, I was forced to withdraw. Someday, I may just complete my MBA.

I was born in downtown Los Angeles, California (I will not tell you good folks in what year), during an earthquake, at the famous old California Medical Center by the 110 Harbor and the 10 Santa Monica Freeways.

This makes me a native Californian. People from California seem to move out of this state, and then people from out-of-state seem to want to move here. This does not make a lot of sense to me. I'm not sure what a native is, however, some people are very impressed when they find out that I am one.

I have traveled quite a bit; however, I have never found any place around the globe that I like better than right here. Maybe that is what a 'native' is—someone who likes it right here in sunny Southern California.

I love Los Angeles, I really truly do. Was its Randy Newman who sang the song, "I Love LA"? I don't recall anymore. Do you?

Furthermore, I want to inform you readers that we really never have major earthquakes in Southern California. They only happen in Northern California, San Francisco are, and the Mammoth Mountain area in the High Sierra's, or the Mojave Desert.

Some people back east believe they happen in LA all the time, but that is just a modern-day myth. Los Angeles is the City of

Angels and they do not allow anything more than a gentle rolling in their town.

TABLE OF CONTENTS

Introduction.. 1

Chapter One—I Love LA 5

Chapter Two—Dimonds are Forever.. 18

Chapter Three—For the Love of Money.................................. 36

Chapter Four—Like a Needle in a Haystack 55

Chapter Five—Follow the Money... 66

Chapter Six—You Can Take That to the Bank.......................... 81

Chapter Seven—Criminals Live Like They Are
Never Going to Die 97

INTRODUCTION

The suspenseful book, *The Eiger Sanction*, by Mr. Whitaker, in 1972, was made into a film in 1975 by the well-known actor and director, Clint Eastwood. Mr. Whitaker has been compared to Ian Fleming, the creator of 'James Bond'.

My name is Charles Warner Kennedy O'Brien, Private Investigator in the City of Los Angeles, California. I am a Detective, albeit, I am the first to admit not a perfect one. LA is my beat, but I have been known to travel all over the United States, and even around the world to solve criminal cases involving white collar crime.

Bank fraud, corporate greed. These cases are often referred to me in lieu of the FBI (Federal Bureau of Investigation), the LAPD (Los Angeles Police Department), Interpol in Europe, or several other investigative organizations.

When I was young, I would guess that like a lot of you young male readers, I read books, listened to the radio, and studiously watched police detectives and PI's (Private Investigators) on television and at the movies, solve their ever -baffling cases.

There was the wise old Charlie Chan, Sherlock Holmes, and Dr. Watson, Mike Hammer, Raymond Chandler, Colombo, Phillip Marlow, Barretta, Raymond Novaro, Joe Friday in Dragnet. Jack Webb was a great guy, but critics panned him as not being a good actor.

The term Dragnet came from the old fishing days around 64 A.D. They were great big fish nets they had to drag to bring to shore. Hence, the term 'Dragnet'.

And, there was always Ian Fleming's James Bond, always one of my and many other people's favorite spies. Others were Mannix, Mike Connors, Hawaii Five-O, Jack Lord, Kojak, Telly Savalas, and many other detectives and PI's from the good old days. Also, Magnum PI (new one and old).

Other recent favorite detectives or Private Investigators are on the shows, CSI-Las Vegas (or Lost Wages as some people call Vegas), CSI-Miami, David Caruso is just perfect for the Horatio Cain detective role in my opinion, CSI-New York—the CSI Trilogy, I believe they call it.

And, Law and Order, Law and Order Special Victims Unit (SVU), and Law and Order Criminal Intent. There's also The Mentalist, The Medium, Without a Trace, Cold Case, Leverage, Southland, Dark Blue, Psych.

And, In Plain Sight, Jason Bourne (Matt Damon), Person of Interest, Homeland, Covert Affairs, Justified, Crossing Lines, The Bridge, Blue Bloods, NCIS (NCIS LA), The Americans, The Mentalist, White Collar, as well as several others.

Now I want to tell you about one of my more harrowing and intriguing cases I have ever worked on. I awoke one night with a .45 caliber automatic Colt model 1911 pistol pointed right in my face.

Actually, I am not afraid of being shot by a 9mm automatic or a .38 revolver, but I know from experience and observation in my past as an LAPD homicide police detective that you do not walk away from a .45 shot to your body and especially one to your head.

I always carry two weapons with me at all times. You never know when you will need an extra, or when one may misfire or jam. I prefer to use a .40 caliber Glock auto pistol (I like the Glock 9mm as well), along with a .38 lightweight LT Smith and Wesson 3" barrel revolver on my ankle under my slacks. It has come in handy on several occasions.

"You are a dead man right now," said the man with the big gun. And then he added, "The Macintosh Independent Bank in Pasadena has put out a contract on you." You might say you're in Pasadena now, as they used to say around this town in the good old days (1970's-1990's).

"I am a hit man. And I really do need the money. This is just what I do. I hope you will not take it personal. It is just business."

Then, I heard a deafening noise that rang in my head, and afterwards a red-hot pain in my right shoulder and left leg. I then I finally passed out on my floor.

When I woke again, I was lying on my back in a ditch in the San Fernando Valley, known to the locals as the *Valley.*

It's part of Los Angeles County, and the people of the Valley hate the City and County of LA. They have been trying to annex themselves from it for many years without any success, yet anyway.

I myself have to admit that I hate the Valley. It is just too hot, it's way too smoggy, it is also too crowded, and its real estate and houses are overpriced ($).

Besides all that, they talk funny out here. You've heard of the Valley Girls, I am sure? That is just one more example of why I live at the beach.

I thought I was going to die for sure. I could not move a muscle when I first came around. The pain was almost unbearable, actually it was unbearable.

Then I crossed my fingers, and said to myself, "If you will save me from this terrible mess, I'm in, I will become a Private Detective that will make my family proud."

He did, of course, and here I am alive and well to tell you about another case I worked on. And it only hurts on cold, wintry days.

PREFACE

You have probably heard the saying all types of dancers use all the time, “I am going to bring it, and I am going to leave it all out on the dance floor.”

Detectives and Private Investigators, both public police detectives and self-employed private detectives and investigators, do pretty much the same thing as the dancers.

The only difference is that sometimes, just every once in a while, these individuals have to leave some of their blood and/or their lives on the floor, on the job. This saying is sort of the private investigators own professional Manta.

Chapter One
I Love LA

I INVESTIGATE EMBEZZLEMENTS in the so called 'too big to fail' banks in the good old USA, as well as in foreign countries all over the globe. On occasion, I also investigate criminal activities like *Ponzi* schemes.

Think Bernard L. Madoff, 'Bernie' and his 65 *Billion* -dollar rip off, and the unethical stock and investment brokers of Lehmann Bros, AIG, J.P. Morgan Chase, etc.

The other day as I dressed for work, I looked into the mirror. Staring back at me was an extremely handsome, angular man, around 6'4", with a surfer mop of sun kissed hair.

I had preternatural hazel eyes—so intense that when most women looked at me, they had to avert their eyes in embarrassment. Well, to be truthful, at least my eyes are hazel.

I took another look into the mirror just for fun, and I saw a good-looking man with an angular face topped by a nest of naturally wavy black hair and a shy smile that made women swoon—so boyish and charming, yet masculine at the same time. I had a good six-pack, courtesy of crunches and weightlifting at 24-Hour Fitness Center, and a very strict eating regimen.

Then, finally, I realized I was just imagining what I was seeing in the mirror, so I decided to take another look—a harder look this time, a more realistic one. And I saw my real self, I thought anyway.

Appearing in my mirror was a very nice looking, mature gentleman with a full head of hair, albeit some of it was gray. Well, alright, a lot of it was gray. With friendly and warm, yet piercing hazel eyes that sometimes looked blue, other times green like Irish eyes, and sometimes even appeared brown.

I didn't see a six pack this time around—frown. Nor a smile that would make women swoon, I was sorry to admit.

All in all, what I saw in the mirror this time around was a man who had lived a very hard life. I always worked hard, always tried to help those who were less fortunate than myself, and always tried to do my best at whatever task I had before me.

Then I said to myself, "Charlie, you are the man!" And, I turned around and left the bathroom with the image of the *first* man I saw in the mirror still in my mind's eye.

What? You mean to tell me you've never heard of an Irish detective? Well, there are not too many to my knowledge, but there are a few. For example, I am one of them! My name again is "Charles Warner Kennedy O'Brien", but call me Charlie for short.

CHARLIE O'BRIEN: PRIVATE INVESTIGATOR

My mother wanted to name me Alan, but my father won that argument. His father and grandfather were both named Charles. My mother wanted to name me something different. She felt everyone would call me *Good Time Charlie*.

I rarely get called that these days, but I did when I was a kid in school. I never paid much attention to the nickname and it didn't offend me at all. I am mostly Irish, with some British and Norwegian mixed in for a good sense of humor.

I am currently buying a very nice office condominium in an expensive high-rise building, the Traveler's Insurance Building on Wilshire Boulevard, just west of Downtown LA, just off and north of the 10, Santa Monica Freeway. The offices on Wilshire are expensive, and the prices keep going up, even in this current economic recession—or depression as I call it.

I am a nationally respected PI, with contacts in most major cities in the US. It's a sort of status symbol to have a PI office in this professional area of LA. The only better address for a PI would be Beverly Hills.

Like Anthony *the Pelican* Pelecano used to have before he went away to prison for unlawful detective practices—wiretapping, threats, intimidation—just to name a few of the allegations and convicted crimes.

Everybody who is anybody in LA knows and respects Wilshire Boulevard. I love LA—I truly do. If you ask me why, I can give you lots of reasons. I've traveled around most of the globe, but

PROFESSOR ALAN DALE DICKINSON

I have never found a place I like or enjoy more than good old Los Angeles in Southern California—I really have not.

As a former LAPD police lieutenant, I worked in the infamous robbery and homicide *Rampart Division* precinct. I was a police detective until my early retirement. Rampart Division is located close to the quaint, beautiful MacArthur Park, named for the courageous General MacArthur from WWII.

The park had a different name when it opened in 1929, but that name has been long forgotten and well before my time.

Across from the park is the famous School of Design, near the man-made lake. Students come to the renowned design school from all over the world to learn design of clothing, homes, automobiles, and many other wonderful things.

I remember playing and boating on the little lake as a child, way back in the day. Wow, I think I must be getting old. What a change in the area from then until now. Unfortunately, today it's a big drug and crime area in LA. There had not been a murder in MacArthur Park for some time—until yesterday.

The new LAPD police headquarters is located nearby at 100 W. 1st Street in downtown LA. East is Main Street, west is Spring Street, and south is Second Street. It's due south of the famous LA City Hall and the 101, Hollywood Freeway.

And, a few blocks south of the recently beautifully restored Union Railway Train Station. The old police building was near Temple Avenue and First Street, one block east of City Hall.

The new police headquarters has half a million square feet of space and cost $437,000,000 to build the state-of-the-art police complex. It's a good thing the LAPD executives got the funding for the building several years ago, back when the city was not so financially broke. If they had waited until today, the complex would not be approved for many years to come.

The building stands ten stories high—and is a truly amazing structure to behold. The old police headquarters was just eight stories with 398,000 square feet, and cost just six million to construct in 1955. In 1966, it was named after Police Chief William (Bill) H. *Parker*, after his death.

The old building was very modern for its time—it boasted modernist design lines, expanses of glass, walls and columns accented with mosaic tile, and interior walls and partitions that could be moved and would lend future flexibility to the building's occupants.

It also had super-secret electronic microphones in the jail cells and interview rooms, and telephone tap devices. Also revolutionary for its time back in 1955, an entire floor was dedicated for use as a crime lab, like you see in the CSI series on TV today.

It was equipped for sophisticated chemical testing and was filled with state-of-the-art scientific equipment. The old building even had an LAPD helicopter landing pad on the roof.

PROFESSOR ALAN DALE DICKINSON

I attended the LAPD training academy located close to the famous Dodger baseball stadium in Chavez Ravine, just off the 5 Freeway heading to the San Fernando Valley and Central and Northern California.

At LAPD, I worked for the then Chief of Police, Bernard C. Parks. He was one of the best police chiefs we have had in LA—one of the most efficient police chiefs anywhere in the world. Now, he is a dedicated active member of the LA City Council.

And, I hope he will soon be elected to higher political office. I voted for him in an election for LA County in which he narrowly lost. Mr. Park's professionalism, high ethics, and great character are such that he did not make a big deal for a recall after the election.

I am 99% certain that all law enforcement officers in LA, and elsewhere in the US, are very honest, hardworking, dependable, willing to risk their lives on a moment's notice, caring and trustworthy, among many other fine, admirable qualities.

There's always a bad apple in every bunch, however, as the old saying goes. Unfortunately, I am sorry to say, you may have heard about the Rampart scandal years ago, when there were some bad apple detectives became worse than the criminals, they were supposed to protect the public from. I knew some of those bad cops—and I helped put some of them away.

Something I like to do when pondering a PI case I 'M working on—like the one I am about to tell you about—is to ride the famous *Angel's Flight* tram on Bunker Hill downtown LA. The Flight lift ride was closed for many years in the 1970's-90's due to earthquake damage.

Yes, we do have *some* earthquakes here in sunny Southern California, I am sad to admit. But since LA is *City of Angels,* they do watch over us and try to make most of the quakes just like a little rolling thunder, and not too terribly detrimental.

I am so glad the Flight re-opened. I rode on it when I was a little kid and it brings back old memories of days gone by. I have an old picture of it somewhere. If I can find it, I think I'll get it framed and put it on the wall of my new PI office on Wilshire Boulevard.

The Flight is located just east of the very old Crocker Bank headquarters building that's no longer in business. Crocker Bank went out of business years ago due to poor management and lack of capital. The three-building cluster is done in brown brick and marble, and is still a beautiful structure.

It's a real shame that a lot the outstanding banks of LA are now a thing of the financial past in the banking capital of the West coast, including LA and San Francisco.

Wonderful banks helped build the LA of today. Banks helped so many men and women and small businesses to spread out all over downtown, including banks like Security Pacific National Bank, First Interstate Bank, Quaker Bank, and of course, many smaller banks that have now disappeared too—way too many to list here.

I live in Hermosa Beach. The word means *beautiful* in Spanish. Hermosa Beach is located near Santa Monica, Redondo Beach, Manhattan Beach, and is not far from the lovely Marina Del Rey. I can walk to the majestic Hermosa Pier, to the Pacific Ocean, and to the fancy restaurants and quaint little shops and small pubs in the area—and these are all wonderful to see!

I love to drink iced-tea—but not the Long Island kind. And, every once in a while, I will instead order a big glass of milk for my ulcer. People often gasp' when they see a grown man drinking cow juice in a bar.

Another reason I don't drink much alcohol anymore is that my memory is getting so bad that if I drank, I probably would not be able to find my way home!

My home is a gorgeous beach house off the strand. I love to watch the healthy young women playing volleyball and walking out onto the famous pier. I wish I had a hard body like some of the guys on the beach have. Even when I was younger, I don't think I was ever in as good shape as they are.

Oh, to be youthful once again! I try not to stare at the lovely young ladies in their almost non-existent bikinis. I succeed in this most of the time. We men should not lust, as you know, but since I am human and a red-blooded male, I have to admit that I sneak a peek or two—or three—every once in a while.

I assume that most men around here do the same. Yes, I still like to look at the pretty, athletic women. But at my ripe old age, I sometimes forget why I am looking!

You should know, there are some of the most beautiful women in the world right here in sunny Southern California. Well, also in Roma (Rome), Italy, something I noticed when I spent a month in Rome in 1996. The place was absolutely wonderful, marvelous, and breathtaking. And the sightseeing was out of this world.

I do get lonely sometimes, like most other PI's I am sorry to confess. It's an occupational hazard. But I am never *really* alone. I have Someone looking out for me, keeping watch to make sure than none of the bad guys I am investigating take me out of action while I am ferreting out white collar embezzlement crime in LA and other cities around the world.

They say the *beautiful* people in LA live mostly in Beverly Hills, Bel Air, and Hollywood. Hollywood is sometimes referred to as *Holly-weird* by some of its detractors. Other places to find the beautiful people is Santa Monica, Malibu, that Fairfax district, and Laguna Beach, among others.

Some even live right downtown LA now, by City Hall or the Staples Center where the Lakers play basketball for the NBA. They live in lofts newly converted from old apartment buildings. There are lots of lofts spread out around LA these days. And you can buy one fairly cheap right now due to the real estate recession—or depression as I call it.

PROFESSOR ALAN DALE DICKINSON

I have always preferred to live by the beach. My beloved mother felt the same way, and that's where I got it from. I miss her a lot these days. She's buried out by the famous Malibu movie Colony where a lot of movie stars and business Titans or TV personalities live.

My parents lived in the Malibu area before I was born and knew many of the movie stars of the 1940s era. My father was the restaurant manager at the fabulous Malibu Inn, right next to the beautiful Malibu Pier.

In the heart of Malibu, just up from the Surf Rider Beach, is the famed Malibu Movie Colony—a half mile small stretch of one hundred or so homes that sit just inches apart on the beautiful Pacific Ocean shoreline.

The roster of its residents reads like the credits of the world's largest ensemble movie. And the price tags start in the low millions and go up from there—way, way up.

Mrs. May Knight Rindge, widow of the industrial millionaire Frederick Rindge, was left the sole owner of the 17,000-acre Malibu Ranch, as it was originally named in 1905. The seaside paradise stretched from Las Flores Canyon to the Ventura County line.

She fought development and expansion. Only the US Supreme Court Washington DC forced her eventually to allow the Pacific Coast Highway to be built through her beloved Malibu Rancho.

When she finally offered development, she offered ten-year leases on a stretch of coast just west of the exquisite Malibu Pier to anyone willing to build a house on the land. The thirty-foot lot cost $30 per month, or $1 per beach foot.

It is almost unimaginable today to believe that this pristine land was so inexpensive at one point in time. I guess that is what the word *inflation* means.

Among those first to lease in the movie colony was Swedish silent film star, Anna Q. Nilsson. Then came Delores del Rio, Bing Crosby, Clara Bow, Gary Cooper, Barbara Stanwyck, and Ronald Coleman.

Mrs. Rindge was a teetotaler—she drank no alcohol. So, she wrote restrictions into each lease stating that if anyone was caught drinking, their lease and the house they had built with their own money could be taken back by her. This was about 1926 or so—around the time of prohibition.

By 1938, Mrs. Rindge was broke, unfortunately, due to the Depression of 1929-1934, and she was forced to file for bankruptcy—similar to what we see happening today. Then, in the early 1940's, the empty lots in the colony were sold for $6,000 to $15,000. Rents back then ranged from $37 to $100 per month. Today, those same rents are $50,000 and up—way up.

Those beach shacks back then were a bit flimsy. One Malibu Beach historian said, "You could almost push your finger right through the walls."

Another said, "It was impossible to breathe in one house and not cough up carbon dioxide in another next door."

Today, some of the famous VIP's who live (or have lived) in the beach houses in this stretch include: Tom and Rita Hanks, Kevin Kline, Larry Hagman, Frank Capra, Linda Ronstadt (the famous singer and ex-girlfriend of the well-known California politician Jerry Brown, son of Pat Brown, Governor of California back in the day)

And there's Alice Cooper, Cher (of Sonny and Cher fame), Liz Taylor and Richard Burton, Don Rickles (comedian), and Robert Redford. This list of names just barely scratches the surface of famous Malibu residents.

The remarkable actress, Ms. Collin 'Wilcox' Paxton lived in the Colony until 1977. She starred in the Oscar winning film, *To Kill a Mockingbird*, with Gregory Peck, directed by the well-known Robert Mulligan.

She had numerous roles on TV series, including The Twilight Zone, The Fugitive, Dr. Kildare, Gunsmoke, and The Walton's. She also appeared in several movies, like Catch 22 and Jaws 2. She loved her ocean front Malibu home, but when she retired from acting, she moved back to her beloved home in the high-lands of South Carolina.

I was married for thirty-three years, once upon a time. My cute former spouse decided all of a sudden to desert me for another man. It was kind of a shock to me, as you might well imagine.

Some of my friends and relatives referred to her as the *Wicked Witch of the West*, from the *Wizard of Oz*, the movie starring Judy Garland from the Golden Age of Movies. That description is possibly a little harsh, however, who knows a better one? I survived.

I like to drink a big glass of grape juice every once in a while. The doctors say it is good for my ulcer and high blood pressure. Grape juice, and even a little red wine, are best for what ails us.

Most of my friends drink a little beer or wine, but none of them drink very much. However, some of my PI clients drink—and some, quite a bit. Mostly, it's wines from well-known wine presses.

One very special wine they have shared with me is the 2006 Chateau Andrea Cabernet Sauvignon, from Paso Robles, CA. This is from one of the warmest wine regions, just perfect for producing powerfully fruit driven cabs like the award-winning Chateau Andrea. It is perfect with a steak dinner.

Also, there's the 2008 Domaine Lalande Pinot Noir, OC, VdP from France—the spiritual home of Pinot Noir. In the hot south, you still get the famous haunting aromas, but also an added fruity richness.

A juicy and spicy classic from one of the famous estates is the 2006 Burley Fox Shiraz from Eastern Australia. It is a terrific example of why this style of deep, dark, Aussie Shiraz is hugely popular right now. It has layers of black cherry fruit with spicy notes—a special deluxe cuvee from a top producer.

The 2007 Chateau Grand Jour, Bordeaux Sperieur, AOC, is an intense fruit rich Bordeaux Sperieur, a cut above, from the tiny Chateau in the heart of the world's greatest wine region in France.

You should taste why these reds inspire such devotion among wine lovers everywhere.

Then, there's the 2007 La Revelation Sauvignon Blanc, Bordeaux, AOC, from France. As I discovered, 2007 was a great year for Bordeaux Sauvignon. It's refreshing, sleek, and loaded with fresh pear flavors. It's a smart choice for seafood dinner or as the first cool glass after a long, hard day at work.

There's the 2007 Los Rosales Chardonnay, Ropel, from Chile. Its gold-medal quality shines through in every glass of this wonderfully pure, gently oaken Chardonnay. Established way back in 1824, this historic estate is at the forefront of Chilean winemaking.

Pinot Grigio is big at the moment, but for a maximum of flavor in this variety you need to head to Italy to taste the 2007 Villa Masetti Pinot Grigio, Venzie, IGT, Italy. You will find few better wines than this crisp aromatic white from this stunning estate near Venice—the beautiful city on the water. It is great wine with almost any food.

There's also the 2007 Oakton Lane Chardonnay, San Luis Obispo, California. It's ripe, fresh, bursting with tropical fruit. Oakton Lane is a modern California wine. San Luis Obispo in central California is one of *the* places for wine right now.

My clients know that I do not drink much, but very selectively. In the old days when I was younger, people were not as understanding about drinking. Also, I really like to dance. I can still 'get down' even though I am a little bit past my Prime.

So, it's quite alright with me if you are going to dance, but the moral of this story is to please be sure you are fully clothed before you get down and bust a move!

I know it must sound strange for an older PI like me to enjoy driving a classic 1964 Chevy Impala 2-door hardtop Super Sport on weekends when I have time off between criminal cases.

It has a 409 cubic inch V-8 engine, four on the floor gearshift with a chrome knob, a posi-traction rear end differential, and Crager magnesium wheels from the 1960's.

It's a beautiful deep maroon color with jet black bucket seats. The whole car is in *mint* pristine condition. Who knows its current value in the depressed worldwide market, but it's worth is estimated at seventy-five thousand dollars.

The 1964 Chevy Impala is one of the finest cars General Motors ever made. The only possible exception is the 1957 Chevy Bel Air 2-door coupe with the small block and mighty 283 cubic inch engine, preferably black in color with lots of chrome showing.

A couple of good years for the older Corvettes were notably the beautifully detailed 1967 Corvette Stingray 427 Roadster. It is perhaps one of the most collectible cars ever produced in the US.

Powered by the legendary 427 cubic inch 390 hp V-8 engine with a 4-speed manual transmission, the nut and bolt matching number came with tuxedo black seats and attention-grabbing red stinger hood accent and a convertible top—definitely a long lived and proven classic vehicle.

Speaking of Chevy Corvettes, I am thinking of buying a new Corvette myself. A ZR-1 model is one of the fastest cars on the road, but it eats up a lot of gas and money. I found one that had original signatures of some key Corvette executives inside the hood, which make this an instant
collectible classic automobile. But I had to pass on purchasing it. They wanted $100,000 cash for it. And that was way over my budget. I guess I will have to keep on looking.

For now, I will keep on driving my BMW 750-IL V-10, which is one of the finest road production vehicles in the whole world.

I also like to drive my classic 'Chevy to the levy' and down Whittier Boulevard in East LA on Saturday nights. There are some absolutely fabulous rides in East LA—some of the finest in the whole country. Their cars can do all sorts of tricks, like jumps and bounces, U-turns, and spins. Absolutely terrific vehicles, they really are.

And, when I have extra time off hard working my PI cases, if you can call being a PI hard work, I will drive my classic Chevy all the way from Santa Monica at the Pacific Ocean to Chicago, Illinois along the famous Route 66.

When I am cruising the boulevards and highways in my classic Chevy, I listen to my oldies but goodies songs on my satellite car radio or my iPod.

Remember Mr. Art Laboe, the famous disc jockey from LA? Well, he did a live album concert at the famous El Monte Legion Stadium in El Monte, CA. It is one of the best I have ever heard, then or since, from that early era. This stadium is one of the original roots of LA's Rock n' Roll.

Songs from the album and the artists who performed at that time years ago were: The Penguins, Don Julian and the Meadowlarks, Marvin and Johnny, handsome Jim Balco, Earth-Wind-and Fire, The Shields, Rene and Rene, Sonny Knight, the Galahad's. And, the Pentagons, the Jaguars, Ron Holden, Tower of Power, Pete Wingfield, Billy Stewart, the Intruders, the Hitmakers, the fabulous Brenton Wood, and Chuck Higgins.

Many of you readers may not be old enough to remember these absolutely incredible early Rock n' Roll classic entertainers, but many of you have probably heard their songs on your iPods, CD's, internet radio, or another venue. I certainly hope so!

The Penguins did the song *Earth Angel,* a huge classic. Sonny Knight did *Dedicated to You.* Marvin and Johnny did the fabulous *Cherry Pie.* And one of my all-time favorites, The Intruders, did *I Will Always Love My Mama*—a song that is even more relevant to me today than it was way back then when it was originally recorded.

Pete Wingfield did *Eighteen and a Bullet.* And the Shields did *You Cheated, You Lied.* There was the popular *Lo Mucho Que Te Quiero* by Rene and Rene. The Hitmakers did *Chapel of Love.* Chuck Higgins sang the *Pachuko Hop,* a very popular dance song in Southern California.

The marvelous Earth-Wind-and Fire did *Reasons.* And last but not least, the Penguins mesmerized their listening audience with their special rendition of *Memories of El Monte* and Legion Stadium.

While reminiscing about music, I received a frantic call from the IBBC Bank—The International Business Banco Corporation.

It was the Executive Vice President on the phone, a Mr. Carlos Gerald 'Jerry' Frankhoffer saying, "We have a problem!"

The large bank is located in LA at the corner of Third and Hope Streets. I know it well because it is a beautiful fifty-five story high rise located right in the middle of LA's financial district on top the famous Bunker Hill.

I remembered its five-star restaurant complete with a top gourmet French chef and an experienced large staff. This fine eating establishment is located in the building on the fifty third floor. I had the occasion to dine there many times with clients. The food was sublime and the service impeccable.

I also remembered the gorgeous art collection located one floor up from the restaurant on the fifty fourth floor of the IBBC Bank Building. It is an expensive and expressive art collection of the finest quality, with well-known oil paintings worth several million dollars.

The breathtaking art collection flashed through my mind—Vincent Van Gogh, the Dutch master, Harmenzoon Van Rijn or 'Rembrandt', the Dutch Illusionist, Paul Gauguin, French Post-Impressionist, Pablo Picasso, Spanish Cubist, Jackson Pollack, American Abstract Impressionist.

And, Salvador Dali, Spanish Surrealist and several other French masters like Henry Matisse, Claude Monet, Edgar Degas, Pierre Auguste Renoir, Paul Cezanne.

And Gustav Klim, Art Nouveau, Georgia O'Keefe, American Modern Artist, and Rogier van der Weyden, Dutch. Yes, the art had made an impression on me.

Other works they held were Wassily Kandinsky, Russian Abstract, Mark Rothko, Expressionist, Marc Chagall, Russian Modernist, Paul Gogan—and an array of lesser known fine artists who produced magnificent works, I thought.

IBBC Bank also had some exquisite statues and sculptures on display at that fifty fourth floor I recalled. One was by the multi-talented and unsurpassed genius of Leonardo Da Vinci, Italian Renaissance master.

On the top floor, the fifty fifth, were the bank executive offices, including the offices of the Board of Directors. I knew the Chairman of the Board recently moved his office to the London IBBC Bank for international banking reasons.

IBBC in LA had spared no expense on the office décor. I heard each of the offices was said to have cost one million dollars to furnish.

The bank has several offices in major US cities and also overseas in London, Paris, Geneva, Hong Kong, Tokyo, Dubai—just to name a few of the top locations.

The IBBC's LA bank building was built in 1974 at a cost of $100,000,000. One hundred million was a lot of money back then. But the bank was very prudent and made lots of money in 1980 by selling the structure to an east coast life insurance company—AIG—for a sum of $300,000,000. The IBBC leased back the space from AIG at a very low cost per square foot.

The IBBC bank has one of the best views in LA. "On a clear day you can see forever..." like the song says. You can see the San Gabriel Mountains to the northeast and the breathtakingly beautiful Pacific Ocean to the southwest.

Of course, when it is smoggy, you can barely see the rest of LA. But I think the air quality is getting a lot better in LA now.

The panicked voice of Jerry from IBBC on the phone continued, "Seventy-five million dollars went missing from the bank's central cash vault in our basement!"

I thought to myself, Charlie, "That's a whole lot of money! Not what I would call peanuts, particularly in today's horrible economic climate."

"The actual cash is not missing from the vault of course. It must have occurred through an electronic funds transfer (EFT), with someone debiting a very large cash account," I offered.

I went on, "I know how secure your vault is and no one could carry out that kind of cash from such a secure vault in an attaché case."

Jerry said firmly, "Neither the LAPD nor the FBI has been brought into this. That's the way we want it."

The Board of Directors wants to keep this all-in house, if at all possible," he went on. "They are concerned about bad publicity—a public relations nightmare for the IBBC Bank."

As he spoke, I thought it might be too early to tell, but I had the sense that he was in my words: *JDLR.* That's my acronym for *Just Doesn't Look Right.* He could very well be the perpetrator! Just a thought that crossed my PI mind.

"The bank is sincerely worried that if the public were made aware of something like this theft or embezzlement of this magnitude, there would be a run on the bank. In this day and age, with the US banking industry in a meltdown stage, we would be put right out of business. That or the Federal Deposit Insurance Corporation (FDIC) would shut us down," Jerry said.

I knew that the LAPD leaks like a sieve when it comes to scandals, high profile murders, celebrity arrests, bank problems, and the like. Now I love the police department and served them well, but leaks are a fact of life in LA.

You can't go to the grocery store without seeing the latest scandals splashed across the gossip rags—Mel Gibson's case, Paris Hilton's traffic court incident, TV Barretta star Robert Blake's murder-for-hire allegations.

And I thought of cases like the music innovator and record producer of the famous John Lennon and the Beatles, the Phil Spector case. The John and Kate plus eight, the tragic early death of

Michael Jackson—murder, suicide, or just plain medical negligence? Only the District Attorney may know for sure.

As Jerry talked anxiously, I thought how there are so many notorious LA publicity leaks and I said to him, "Well I certainly empathize with the bank's vivid concerns about bad publicity, however, I feel I should strongly advise you to immediately notify the LAPD and the FBI, and possibly even Interpol at once."

After we hung up, I thought long and hard about what I had already heard of Mr. Carlos Gerald 'Jerry' Frankhoffer, aka *The Jackal*.

He's on the Board of Directors at the ICCB Bank and very well connected, as they say. He knew all the right influential board directors. If he were not in such an enviable position, he would have been fired a long time ago. I heard he was a terrible manager and boss.

He's personally in charge of 1,600 branches or offices around the world, with about 125,000 associates or employees. He is mostly bald and stands just five feet tall, with lifts in his shoes, and he weighs about 110 pounds. He's a small man outwardly—and even smaller on the inside.

Carlos, *The Jackal*, as his detractors refer to him, reminds me of the actor-turned-politician, Arnold B. Schwarzenegger in his role as the *Terminator.* The *Jackal* is the *Terminator* of the IBBC bank, or at least that is the role he seems to adopt when dealing with staff.

He sees his primary job to fire as many people as he possibly can. He loves—I do mean loves—to zap or terminate long term employees when at all possible. And his favorite victims are those closest to retirement and their well-earned full benefits.

I was told that many felt Carlos was so mean spirited, cold, and hateful because he was very small in stature—and not all that bright or intelligent. They say he has a Napoleon complex due to his small size. Who knows? I'm not sure what kind of complex he has, but he seems to have some kind of personality disorder.

Carlos has two security guard officers and a chauffeur escorting him whenever he goes outside the big bank building, so he is aware of his enemies. They were all armed, strapped, of course. He hired as bodyguards former LAPD police detectives just like me.

I thought how glad I would be when this case is over and done. Whatever my part in solving it, I hoped to never have to deal with him again.

Yes, I heard that the *Jackal* had many enemies at the IBBC bank. He had enemies both inside and outside the bank's culture. They referred to him as the *Jackal* after the infamous Cuban hit man in the 1980's -1990's. I'm not sure whatever happened to that hit man, and if the CIA or Interpol knows, they are not talking.

And yes, I could empathize. It seemed to me that ulcers go with the territory. All the managers at the bank probably had an ulcer like me, I thought, or a bad heart, or high blood pressure. It comes with the amount of stress associated with working with types like Carlos, the *Jackal*.

Of course, the managers eat too much rich food, complements of their expense accounts. Some drink way too much, although a lot have cut back in recent years. They don't exercise.

And some smoke. A lot have quit smoking lately, thank *God*. Even second-hand smoke kills, as the good doctors and researchers say.

I continued my line of thinking with what I knew about the bankers. They worry way too much. They have a lot of stress. Handling other people's millions can easily give one pause and stress related illnesses.

They have to work on their own personal problems as well as the personal and financial problems of their many and varied customers, managers, and stockholders. And they worry about all the banking regulators and auditors, inside and outside the bank.

I noticed that bankers and other business types don't often go to the doctor for checkups, nor to psychologists for help. This is probably because if anyone found out, that might show weakness. They want to appear totally self-reliant and mentally tough. They tell themselves to "man (or woman) up," as the old cowboy saying goes.

They need to know that seeking help and maintaining overall good health doesn't show weakness. And it doesn't reflect a lack of emotional strength in the least.

But that is how bankers and others like them sometimes perceive it, for some reason. I reason that ego plays a big part in this whole line of thinking.

PROFESSOR ALAN DALE DICKINSON

This new case with the IBBC bank has my mind spinning and my heart pumping fast. And I *pray* it is not my high blood pressure! My palms are sweating and my pulse is racing again—just like in the good old days.

I've often thought, "Oh to be born and to die in LA". That is what I've always believed would happen to me.

Chapter Two

Diamonds are Forever

I made a few discreet inquiries with my local contacts at the LAPD and the LA Sheriff's Department, and calling the New Scotland Yard and MI-5 in Great Britain, and Interpol in Europe.

I determined that someone had recently purchased seventy-five million dollars' worth of raw uncut diamonds of very high quality and good clarity from a questionable gem dealer business entrepreneur outside of Moscow, Russia, in the former Soviet Union, in an area of Siberia known for its diamonds.

It is a very cold part of the country. Bone chilling cold. Indeed.

My sources said the diamond seller was likely the former high-level ranking officer with the formidable KGB—the former Soviet secret police and intelligence agency. I was told that his name was Viktor Kharchenko, nicknamed *The Fisherman*.

He was believed to have a lot of contacts in the underworld in Russia, and around the globe for that matter.

The Fisherman's favorite quote was said to be, "Diamonds are more valuable than cash. They do not fluctuate as badly as cash during financially troubled times. And they are much easier to smuggle into other countries!"

And, he would sometimes add, "Diamonds are forever," just like the James Bond movie.

The questions I began to think about were: a) Who was the buyer of these diamonds, and b) Did he or she work for the IBBC bank? It was no coincidence that the seventy-five-million-dollar price tag matched the amount the bank was missing. And of course, c) How do I find them?

I let these questions into my mind for a while, as I thought of where I usually like to advertise my PI business. I like to use athletic team's media to advertise on a regular basis. It's expensive, but you know the old saying, "You have to spend money to make money."

The teams I like to advertise with include the following:

LA Dodgers-Baseball:
This is a great team and franchise that originally started out in Brooklyn, New York many years ago. 1940's I believe. They moved to LA in the 1950's and things have never been the same since for the City of Angels. It's an award-winning ball club.

LA Angels of Anaheim-Baseball:
This is another terrific ball club with great coaching. They just keep getting better every year since they started in the 1960's. Gene Autry, the famous singing cowboy and actor, used to own

the club and he started it from scratch as an expansion ball club.

It was sold after his death several years ago. They play ball right next to Disneyland in Orange County in Southern California. This is Walt Disney's old stomping grounds from the 1950's.

LA Kings-Ice Hockey:
This ice hockey team plays at the beautiful Staples Center in downtown LA close to the well-known LA Convention Center. It's not far from the famous old Olympic Boxing Arena, just south of the 10 Santa Monica freeway.

Anaheim Ducks-Ice Hockey:
This team plays at the new Honda Center in Orange County, just across the 57 Freeway from the Anaheim Angels baseball field. They were started and previously owned by Disneyland, but are privately owned currently. They are a very good team and getting better every year.

LA Lakers-Basketball:
This world-renowned team usually has the best coaching in the NBA. They win national championships on a regular basis. They also play at the super nice Staples Center in LA. Many famous Hollywood actors pay a lot of money for tickets for the best seats to watch them every year.

LA Clippers-Basketball:
As hard as they try, and they try hard, they do not seem to get any better year after year. They never seem to make a viable

NBA team even when they spend a great deal of money, all they can afford. I hope and pray that someday the Clip's will play better, stronger, and competitively.

I gave a lot of thought to where to advertise. It may seem silly or a bit odd to some, but I like to advertise on the internet, like on Craig's List. I used to advertise in the LA Times, a wonderful newspaper that I love.

I have been reading the Times since the 1950's. But no one reads the newspapers anymore, with the high-tech methods available everywhere. I am afraid the papers will be going out of business, filing for Chapter 11 bankruptcy soon.

Like a lot of papers, the LA Times readership has plummeted to an all-time low. Many formerly world-renowned papers are now out of business. I know you can't stop progress, but I dread the day when you can't even buy a paper at the local newsstand.

I've gotten several good investigative leads from Craig's List. But I have been told by LAPD friends that there are a lot of unscrupulous people advertising on the net without being even legal or bonded, not even licensed private investigators at all.

I figure they want the adventure or the easy money to be gained by fraud. I mused that they probably think of themselves as Mike Hammer, Sam Spade, or Magnum PI—Tom Selleck!

LAPD told me recently, "Most calls these crooked PI's get off Craig's List are for missing person cases. And usually they don't find the missing souls. Some don't even try to locate anyone—they just charge the fee up front."

"You need to be wary of the whole internet thing, not just the PI ads. There are so many criminals on the net, even more bad types than good ones." I was further warned.

I don't use the internet for online dating like some of my friends and acquaintances. An expert told me, "Half the men who advertise on dating websites are already married! So be careful of those types and be careful about the high costs after the free introductory period," he added.

I thought it was about time I got back to the IBBC bank case at hand, after the short reprise of mine. "On the road again..." as the old Willie Nelson country western song goes.

I thought again why they call Viktor Kharchenko, *The Fisherman*. The meaning behind this infamous title is that whenever he got mad, or even suspected betrayal in any way whatsoever from anyone, or if he just 'got up on the wrong side of the bed' you would soon be 'sleeping with the fishes!" Thus, *The Fisherman*.

The mob in New York, Chicago - The Windy City, or Youngstown, Ohio and other places, including LA, used to say 'sleeping with the fishes' meant that you would be dead, period, end of report!

Viktor was fond of saying, "I will not tolerate failure of any type from those who owe me their loyalty and their lives." He was said to have nerves of steel and ice water running in his veins.

A few of Viktor's international criminal associates believed him to be a rational and reasonable man. Little did they know the real Viktor! He had a phalanx full of crooked lawyers in Moscow, Siberia, London, Hong Kong, and Washington, D.C. among other cities. I say crooked lawyers, but is there any other kind? My apologies to any honest attorneys out there.

Viktor's attorneys cost him a great deal of his ill-gotten profits, I thought, but to him it was probably well worth it. I found that he had never been convicted of a crime, but had been charged a grand total of twenty-nine times. Go figure!

I took a collect phone call on a secure line from an old friend of mine at Interpol in Paris, who told me, "The precious gems were cut into one or two carat stones so they would be much easier to fence or sell.

They were all turned into either a) VS-2 or VS-1 on the GIA geologist clarity scale, or b) G, H, or I on the GIA grading scale, or c) other ideal brilliant cut proportions on the chart I gave you."

He went on, "The beautiful diamonds were all cut with: a) binocular microscopes, b) under special ultra-violet light, c) lever ridge gauge micro-measurements and d) compared to other master comparison stones of the finest color and clarity in the world."

And he said, "This is an ideal cut for diamond brilliance, but two other factors may play an important part in their value: the matters of taste and convenience.

And, according to how rough the crystal looks, a deviation in the proportions is sometimes advisable to avoid a slight occlusion. What is important though is that the angles of the 34.5 and 40.75 should stay exactly the same, whatever the change in other proportions."

This is all very technical, I thought, and to me *Diamonds Are Forever* and represent Love. I recalled too how there are other jewels of life that are also nice for a wife, fiancé or girlfriend, like a garnet for 'friendship', peridot for 'good fortune', sapphire for 'truth', aquamarine for 'hope' and 'good health', citrine for 'happiness', and amethyst for 'peace of mind'.

This reminded me of how much I like sapphires. The combination of sapphires and diamonds is really unbeatable for fine women's jewelry. I have realized that jewels, and diamonds in particular, celebrate the powers that gemstones hold, especially over females, since the beginning of time.

While researching information about diamonds and other gems for my case with the IBBC bank, I came across some old tales about certain gems and precious metals having magical powers.

They seem to lift the inner spirit, and change the attitude of the treasures' owners for the better and make their lives more enjoyable. At least that is how I think the fairy tale goes.

I have advised anyone to add a little bit of magic to their love life by gibing a diamond or other precious gem to a loved one, close friend, or family member. I thought of the many pieces of jewelry I have given during my lifetime and how they were received with such happiness and surprise.

One thing I have learned over the years while working near LA's famous Jewelry District for LAPD, is that when you are lucky enough to have a significant other in your life that on special occasions, or just about any other time, give them bling! Bling is what we call the pretty gemstones in LA. I don't know for sure, but I think all women love bling.

I remembered that I am looking for a new receptionist. My former one just got married to a lucky man. She was a sweetheart of a receptionist. I hope there will be another sweet lady interested in the job soon.

I just may shower her with diamonds and sapphires—rings, bracelets, necklaces, toe rings, anklets, earrings, and bling, bling, bling! On the other hand, I would probably just give her a little paycheck with a lot of good wishes. I am just a bit frugal—cheap if I have to admit it.

I am a little picky—a lot picky if I have to tell the truth. I am set in my ways and getting older by the day. It is becoming increasingly difficult to change my ways—just like old dogs. And it is hard to remember sometimes what I did last week, while I recall things from years ago.

PROFESSOR ALAN DALE DICKINSON

Before I return to thinking of my life and death struggles as a PI, I think there must be a nice young woman out there that appreciates that my writing is lighthearted, candid, and sometimes serious—and may be destined for the popular world of fiction.

My mind wandered back to the IBBC case at hand. I was armed with the crucial information now, about the seventy-five million dollars' worth of diamonds—a girl's best friend, as I thought about Marilyn Monroe's movie.

I was carrying my 'friends'—a .40 caliber Glock automatic and a .38 caliber Smith and Wesson police style revolver.

I decided to jump on a jet plane—a Boeing 787 Dreamliner to Mother Russia to do some field work, as we call it in the trade. Took me eleven hours to get from LAX to Moscow, Russia airport, the Lenin Soviet National Airport, with one stopover at JFK in New York.

I recalled that JFK was the namesake for my middle name, Kennedy. Another stopover was London's famous Heathrow Airport in merry old England.

When I finally arrived, I was extremely tired. Jet lag. It would take me a little while to get back up to full speed. Or even two thirds of full speed these days. I took the subway from the airport.

During my long subway ride to the hotel, I thought how the subways in Russia put ours in the US to shame. Theirs are massive, made of marble, with nice stones, pretty rocks, slate, and tile. Theirs are clean and neat, with no graffiti on the walls or in the subway cars.

Theirs do not have the gangs, thugs, young toughs, or drunks like we have in so many of our nation's underground tubes. Each station was individually designed, with a beautiful rotunda that let in light to the tunnels. Quite breathtaking, really.

At one station stop, I got off and purchased a paperback *Russian for Dummies*. I hoped no one would think I was a dummy, I'm not, but I knew I would need the language skills in this book very soon.

From the station, I called an ex-KGB Colonel I know. He had retired, but still kept his ear to the ground, as they say. His name is Alexander (Alex) Smirnov. I found that he was familiar with the diamond deal I was investigating.

"Anything that large, $75,000,000, a lot of people will know about," he said.

He added, "It set off a red flag in various Russian circles, including the FSB", the Soviet intelligence formerly called the KGB.

I arranged to have dinner with Alex at a fine Moscow restaurant that evening, the Socialist Elite Dinner Club. They call dinner Uzhin, supper. I ordered Chaj (tea), Kpustnyj Salat (cabbage salad), Borsch (beet soup), Bifstroganoff (beef stroganoff), and for dessert, Morozhenoye (ice cream). The food was superb and the service top notch.

We caught up on the good old days and what's happening currently. He married his former KGB partner and sweetheart and they have three kids.

Both are very happy to be out of the business. The family is active in their local Russian Boys and Girls Club.

I checked into a suite and checked the internet for my emails, IM's, Facebook, My Space, and my online organizational planner. Then I checked my cell for my voice mails and texts. I went straight to bed early.

The antique bed was wonderful—huge and the mattress extra thick. I thought to myself, "Maybe a Czar once slept on this bed."

Thank God it is over now. But I felt Déjà vu come over me when I awoke during the night with a 9mm Barretta automatic pistol in my face!

My first thought was, "Thank God it is not a .45 caliber automatic!" I remembered an earlier similar incident with a .45 caliber automatic on another case.

Then he added, "Be very careful from now on because *The Fisherman* is no one to mess around with. I know Viktor Kharchenko from personal experience when he and I were both with the KGB. And he is a very bad actor. Avoid him and his henchmen, if at all possible."

I asked, "Alex, would you get me some additional hardware?" I told him, "I want a 9mm automatic pistol, like the one that was shoved in my handsome face last night, an H&K, an SKS automatic rifle, a trusty AK-47, a double barrel sawed off shot gun, and a .357 caliber 6" barrel Smith and Wesson 6-round revolver—Clint Eastwood's *Dirty Harry* character's and my favorite weapon."

And I added, "Just in case you or someone else needs to go with me, I need a few additional men's play toys like a Kel-tecP-3 AT, .380 3" barrel, good back up pistol, ultra lightweight with an easy trigger pull and only 8.3 ounces, and an Astra 400 9mm, and a .38 pistol."

I said, "This unique gun can shoot 9mm or .38 ammunition. It's an older issue, but a good weapon with many varied uses. Also, I need an FNP .45 ACP 15-round magazine. It brings a lot of very serious firepower to an unfriendly gathering."

"And a DS Arms-B&T, TP 9. A 9mm semi-automatic pistol, 5" barrel and overall length of 12. The cartridge carries 30 rounds, which should be plenty for most 'tea parties.'"

Then last but not least, I said, "And a Kimber-Crimson carry 1911, .45 ACP pistol with a 3" barrel because it is light for this type of heavy-duty weapon and weighs only 25 ounces. It has a laser grip and is made in the good old USA. "

"And just for good measure, or good luck, I need four hand grenades. They are great to get a party started and if you get in a real bind, you will scare the heck out of someone without having to shoot or kill them. And that is always a desired outcome for a good PI," I stated.

Alex said, "The arsenal you want will not be a problem. I still know people."

I realized again how nice it is to have friends in a foreign country. I knew it would be very hard, if not impossible, to obtain this stuff without knowing someone with the right connections. Not to mention it would be a lot more expensive.

I bought Alex lunch, Obyed in Russian, for all his help with my 'carry-on luggage'. I had Kvas (a sweet non-alcoholic drink), Salat Olivye (meat salad), Ukha (fish soup), Golubsty (stuffed cabbage rolls), and for dessert Tohrt (chocolate cake).

The food was delicious and the service smart and fast like it used to be in the US. And buying Alex lunch was the least I could do for all his help. I would expense it to the good folks at the IBBC bank, of course.

I said goodbye and *good luck* to my pal, Alex and I disappeared again. I jumped on the Trans-Siberian Railroad and headed to the city of Omsk, Siberia, in the freezing inhospitable part of Northern Russia.

I had a nice private train cabin, small but very clean, comfortable, and nicely furnished. Most other people on the train were packed in like sardines, I observed. I realized they didn't have the rubles to travel with a private cabin.

I thought I picked up two tails following me closely when I got off the Trans-Siberian train. I figured out that one of them was FSB, the new KGB and just as deadly. I was traveling on a US Passport, so I was easy to track in Russia.

Next time I visit, if there is a next time—and I hope not because it is way too cold for me—I will use my Belgium, Italian, or French Passport. The other tail was probably one of Viktor *The Fisherman* Kharchenko's thugs.

When I arrived in the lovely town of Omsk, the capital city of Siberia, it was all covered with snow that looked like a white blanket laid over the town. It took me two days to get there. The train had to go very slowly because of the dangers of very cold weather.

I made some moves after getting off the train, so I lost both of my tails. I am getting older now, but I still have some twists and turns when I need them.

I contacted a woman Alex recommended to me named Natasha. She worked in a local bookstore in Omsk. She also used to work with Alex at the KGB.

Natasha said she is thankful that she's alive after surviving all the craziness she was involved with at the Soviet Union's former intelligence agency. And, she knew Viktor very well.

She told me, "Everyone in the whole district knows Viktor, *The Fisherman,* very well. He's like a local legend—sort of the Russian version of Robin Hood."

She went on, "He's very powerful and is known to be ruthless and cold blooded when he wants to be."

"Viktor owns several diamond mines just outside of Omsk, in Novokuznetsk, Siberia, which is still a part of Russia. And he owns another mine in nearby Mirna City in Eastern Siberia, Northern Russia.

That one is called the Mirna Diamond Mining Complex. It's one of the deepest open working mines in the entire world."

"The area at Mirna gets temperatures ranging between minus 50 and minus 70 degrees Fahrenheit. And the big wind chill factor makes it seem much colder in the winter.

In other seasons, it's not a lot warmer. During the very brief summer, the locals appreciate a little relief from the freezing cold when it gets to about zero degrees to minus 20F."

I thought, "Kind of what we call an Indian summer that lasts two months in the Russian North Pole."

I told Natasha, "I know from my research that precious diamond gem stones have been in Siberia for centuries, however, due to the severe cold and the very difficult mining conditions, former Soviet Union and Russia was not able to mine them until the twentieth century, the early 1900's."

I said, "Prior to that time, Russia had to import their diamonds directly from well-established African gem mines or buy the little beauties from the expensive diamond brokers in Antwerp, Belgium. They control 90% of the world's diamond market from their little corner of the world, and have been doing so forever."

Natasha replied, "Now Russia relishes the fact that they can mine their own stones, as well as export some to the rest of the world making a nice profit for Mother Russia. The US imports a lot of their diamonds from Russia each year."

"These diamond mines are a huge plus to the bedraggled Russian economy, as it is a trading item for them as well as a great cash money maker. Just like America, Russia has to spend a gigantic number of rubles each year for gas and heating oil from the Middle East, mostly from Iran in Russia's case," she said.

My knowledgeable contact, Natasha, went on, "Viktor owns a large diamond mine in central Africa, and many other businesses including snow and ice removal services in Novokuznetsk, Siberia. He also gives a lot of money to local charities."

"He personally provided the funds to build the only hospital in town, Kharchenko General Medical Treatment Center. It's said he likes having his name on the hospital building."

"These gifts and donations of his are not given because he is generous, nor a caring individual. It kept the locals in line and prevented them from reporting his illegal criminal activities to the authorities in Moscow. The local police are on his payroll, so he doesn't have to worry about anything," she added.

Natasha called me later at my hotel. A one star and not as glamorous as my digs in Moscow. She said, "I heard you can get hold of Viktor in a night club in town. It's one of several he owns and it's in the red-light (prostitution) district."

"It's called the Red Comrade. But be careful because it is wild and wooly, and very dangerous for outsiders to visit."

The next night I said some extra *plans* and then 'took my life into my own hands' clubbing to see the notoriously bad Viktor.

When I appeared at the nightclub at about midnight, a very big rough looking bartender named Nikolai Frolov gave me a funny look. Very suspicious I thought.

He almost gagged when I ordered ice tea, plain, and not the Long Island kind. Even in Russia they know the difference. He thought I appeared different.

And everyone else was drinking vodka—Stolichnaya. They don't drink much Smirnoff vodka in Russia. Some drink Russian red wine though.

Well, I thought to myself, this is the former Soviet Union and they make the best vodka in the world here. That's what I'd been told by my father who was a bartender when I was a kid growing up in the suburbs of LA, Venture, Foster Park, and Ojai—famous for its tennis courts, training, and tournaments.

I quickly noticed that this bartender had a shotgun and a 9m pistol under the bar and within easy reach. Most of the night-club clientele, if you could call the rough looking crowd that, looked like they were strapped too. Probably normal for this town, I thought.

I brought along my .40 caliber Glock pistol with its 15-shot magazine under my coat in my shoulder holster as usual. But I switched my trusty .38 caliber 3" barrel revolver, the one I always keep on my ankle, with the brand new .357 Smith and Wesson revolver that I 'd just gotten from Alex.

I think this is one of the best guns ever made. It has six hard-hitting magnum loads, or hollow points, and it has good weight, but not too heavy for the ankle. And, it never jams on you, like a lot of the more popular pistols a lot of people prefer.

I was feeling very nervous and a little worried and I asked Nikolai, the bartender, "Could I please speak to Viktor?"

After a long, hard stare he said, "Talk to this Viktor about what?"

I said, "I'm an old CIA competitor buddy of his from the Cold War and KGB days." Nikolai must have thought this was way too dumb a thing to say if it were not true, or mostly true, so it must not be a lie. Lucky for me.

Nikolai showed me to a spooky back room way down at the end of a long dark corridor. Then he turned right around and without saying a word he left me standing there looking really stupid.

Holding up each door side post were two really big men, mean looking body guards who surprisingly resembled the two thugs who visited and seriously intimidated me at my hotel with the unpleasant gun in the face routine.

When I smiled at them out of nervousness, I am sure, they both frowned at me at the same time as if on cue. Later I learned from Natasha their names were Oleg Kalmanovic, the one who spoke,

and Syeryozha, the one who didn't talk but who didn't need to since he carried the AK-47 around with him.

I would not let the bodyguards search me, even though they insisted, because I did not want them to take away my protection—my guns. I knew that if push came to shove, I very well might need my weapons in a shoot-out. 'OK Corral' style like 1881 Tombstone, AZ, with Wyatt Earp—but right here with my Russian friends.

I was very surprised when they let me in the door to Viktor's office without their required gun search and seizure. I was now in their world, if there was going to be any gun play.

I think they figured the bartender had already checked me and my story out. And, of course, I was sticking to my story.

I noticed on the desk there were large stacks of US $100 bills, weapons, and drugs, and some business papers laying around the office. Just what you might expect in Viktor's domain and sanctum.

I spoke up, "I don't care about any of your illegal activities, even if you are involved in any, nor about your vast worldwide business empire. All I want to know about are the diamonds. Who bought them from you?"

Viktor said, "What illegal activities?" And then he laughed very loudly. His two bodyguards, now inside the room, one on each side of me, laughed just as loud as Viktor. I hadn't realized I made a joke—I sure hadn't intended it that way.

Viktor stared at me for the longest time, a very deadly stare I might add, and it made me more nervous than I already was. He said, "I can't believe that an American ex-CIA agent, or not, would come all the way to my little town in Novokuznetsk, Siberia, way out in the frozen tundra and deep snow."

I think he felt sorry for me, because I knew he was not the least bit intimidated by me or my guns. I saw that he noticed my weapons as soon as I stepped through his office door. He knew his business. That's how he stayed alive and well.

Finally, he said, "Listen very carefully," in surprisingly good English, "because I will only say this once. If you ever dare to come back to my town, I will kill you in the time it takes to have a shot of good Russian vodka."

His two bodyguards smiled widely, as if they hoped I would come back so they could put a bullet in my brain.

Then Viktor added, "Do you understand, Charlie?"

I said thank God under my breath. I breathed a little too loudly, tried not to look as frightened as I was, and then I forced out a response, "Yes, Viktor, I do understand." I added, "Completely," just to be sure he knew I appreciated his real time and life warning.

After the friendly life-threatening word to the wise, Viktor leaned over and whispered to me, "This is off the record, way off the record, right Charlie?"

I nodded because I couldn't speak with my voice all shaky. He said, "I have indeed sold seventy-five million dollars in previously uncut, but now brilliantly cut, diamonds. I sold them to an IBBC bank executive who works out of the San Diego regional office."

Viktor did not know the man's real name. "I am sure he used an alias like John Smith or something. I never met the man in person, and the whole transaction was consummated over my encrypted cell phone," he said.

"I heard the man may still be in Moscow or Minsk here in the former Soviet Union, but I don't really believe it, he finished."

After he spoke, I immediately began to back out of the room very, very slowly. I did not want to startle the two bodyguards who looked a bit edgy. Both of my hands were ready to reach—for my .40 caliber Glock automatic, right hand, and my new .357 Smith and Wesson Magnum revolver, left hand, with the hollow point rounds I had added for Viktor and this special occasion.

I thought that if I died here, I would take down at least three of the five Russians with me.

I smiled at my two friends holding up the door side posts as I passed them exiting Viktor's office. They gave me another dirty look, which I had gotten used to, and I moved quickly to the bar.

I thanked Nikolai Frolov the bartender for his assistance and I gave him a big tip in US dollars. I thought it would have been cheaper to tip in rubles, but I appreciated that I would never have gotten to speak with Viktor, nor would I have gotten the valuable information about the sale of diamonds to the IBBC bank executive, without Nikolai trusting me.

I said, "Take care of yourself and your family and Mother Russia." And I added, "Dasvidaniya (goodbye)." I was very surprised when he turned and gave me a big smile. You never know when a random act of kindness will be greatly appreciated.

After I left the dark, dank, dangerous, and deadly bar of Viktor's in Omsk, Siberia still alive, I was contacted by the CIA in Langley, Virginia. It was Howard Wallace, a Scotsman I could tell by his voice. He called me via his secured encrypted satellite phone line.

He said, "I have just spoken with your Russian friend, Alexander (Alex) Smirnov, and to your acquaintance at Interpol in Paris. The IBBC told us you are working on a very sensitive internal bank matter for them concerning a missing seventy-five million dollars, or diamonds."

He went on, "While you are in the former Soviet Union, the CIA wants you to go to the Chernobyl Nuclear Power Plant in the city of Pripyat, Ukraine."

"As you know, it is the site of one of the biggest nuclear disasters in the history of the world, and it occurred at this plant on April 26, 1986. It's located not far from where you are now."

I told Howard yes, because I was not quite ready to fly home yet, and for the CIA I would do almost anything. Well, I had turned down some 'wet work' assassinations before.

I recalled the Soviet Union's news media at the time and it said that 56 people had died in the Chernobyl disaster, and another 600,000—over half a million—people suffered from radiation poisoning during the horrific power plant meltdown.

From what I also read in secret papers released from Russia, there were actually 700 people killed and over 1,000,000 (one million) individuals with radiation problems that have led to

severe health difficulties and many premature deaths. I knew this was a very sad chapter in the world's nuclear energy program—worse than most people even know.

The CIA told me, "We want someone there who is not employed by the US Government directly. Go and get a firsthand update on how things are now at the permanently defunct power plant today, in real time. We have not sent an official US delegation there for more than six years, due to the freeze in US and Russian relations."

Howard went on, "Charlie, the IAEA Energy Agency in Vienna, Austria, has been there more recently, however, a lot of their reports were classified "Top Secret" and we have not been able to get our hands on them."

The CIA quickly got me access to the Chernobyl plant through some old connections they still maintained from the good old KGB days.

When I arrived at the plant, I suited up in a very new, space-age looking safety suit, head to toe, with an oxygen tank on my back and large filters on both sides, front and back.

I had arrived there before my Russian escorts, and when they came in and saw me suited up, they laughed. One said, "Charlie, the radiation levels are down now to acceptable levels for humans and animals."

I thought, yeah, right. I was not born yesterday. He added, "You don't really need to wear the Mars space suit."

But I was a little bit, well a lot, worried when they told me this information because I had seen a lot of photos from the nuclear meltdown disaster from back in 1986. And I had also seen several pictures from more recent years of Chernobyl.

The IAEA had taken many photos over the years, and the ones I saw were absolutely devastating. Almost unbelievable. This was a gigantic man-made disaster that never should have happened, as scientists I have spoken to over the years agreed. But after my short panic and worry mode, and at their strong suggestion, I took off my safety suit and said a little *thank you.*

I'd kind of liked the way I looked in the suit—all warm and toasty too. But they said they kept the safety equipment on hand for extra protection just in case something was to go wrong. That was not a very reassuring comment.

After spending all day with them, walking, riding, and examining the totally devastated Chernobyl plant, I said my thank you and Poka, goodbye, to my new Russian friends. They had been very helpful, candid, and courteous to me, even though they probably thought full well in their opinion that I was an 'ugly American'.

I immediately called Howard at the CIA on my encrypted cell phone when I got back into my rental car. It was a nice Lada sedan and handled like a really nice car should.

Before I headed back to my hotel, I reported to Howard on the cell phone: "The air at the plant seemed fine. I didn't have any trouble breathing the natural Chernobyl air. The Geiger counter reflected safe levels of radiation."
"There are live trees, grass, bushes, and weeds growing in and around the old deserted buildings. And local farmers are supposedly not getting sick all the time like they did for many years following the tragedy."

He replied, "All this is very good news, Charlie, but we must remember that the ground there will still be contaminated with radiation for the next six thousand years—should the world last that long."

I remembered that I had not had time yet to read my new little book, *Russian for Dummies*, and I realized I had better start on it soon. I had no idea what most Russian people were saying to or about me, except the ones who spoke English, of course. Luckily for me, a lot of Russians speak English for some reason.

After my informative, but unnerving, visit to Chernobyl Nuclear Power Plant, I called my dependable Russian pal, Alex. I told him thank you and Dasvidaniya (goodbye). Then as soon as I got to Moscow, I jumped on a jet place.

PROFESSOR ALAN DALE DICKINSON

I was anxious to follow up on the case of the IBBC bank embezzlement with the latest information I'd obtained from Viktor, *The Fisherman*, in Omsk.

That's what I will follow up on when I get back to my beloved Los Angeles, after I finish thawing out from the almost unbelievable cold of Siberia in Mother Russia. Thankfully, I was still alive.

Chapter Three

For the Love of Money

AS SOON AS I got back to LA and after I got caught up on my much-needed sleep, the time zone changes of eleven hours, and the jet lag, I called the IBBC bank to report in and update them on all that I had learned in Mother Russia.

Also, I submitted my expense account claim of $25,000. First class travel and necessary weapons for personal protection are not cheap, as you probably know.

Now I needed some time off the case to do some very necessary research about money in general, and the *love of money* in particular. Plus, I need to make some phone calls, personal contacts, and listen to some good old Rock 'n Roll music.

I knew that the rest period would help this old brain, and I believed that studying and making contacts would help me understand and solve the case for the IBBC bank and its shareholders or stockholders.

All that the Federal Deposit Insurance Corporation (FDIC) and the US government and the general public needed right now right smack dab in the middle of the worst economic financial meltdown since 1929 would be another bank failure, right? There were 172 bank failures in 2009 alone.

I just read the other day while doing some research on the love of money, that the root cause of all kinds of greed and evil is the love of money. An old quote says, "Some people are so eager for money [that green stuff] have wandered from their personal beliefs of right and wrong and have wounded themselves with many and serious pains and problems."

I decided to call an old friend of mine to assist me on my bank case. His name is Raymond, *Big Ray,* Chandler. No, not any of the famous detectives or relatives' namesakes, just so happens by a twist of fate to have the same name.

He used to be an insurance investigator in Orange County, California, *the OC* for Aetna Healthcare, Blue Shield, Cigna, or one of the big national insurance companies. He investigated Worker's Compensation cases, sometimes called 'slip and fall cases.

His job was to weed out employees or customers who were really hurt and who needed and deserved financial assistance, from those who were not hurt but who just pretended to be injured and wanted the money in order to quit working and stay at home taking it easy.

Big Ray is a PI now, just like me. He does a lot of work for the insurance industry, since he knows it so well, and for some huge legal firms and large banks.

The reason I call him Big Ray is because he is 6'9". That's pretty big, don't you think? He was a great basketball player in high school, an all-conference player, and he also played at the Chapman University in Orange County, California.

He was born and raised in Hermosa Beach (beautiful in Spanish), close to the lovely pier and just off the famous strand (boardwalk) that parallels the beautiful Pacific Ocean.

Ray just completed some investigative work for the Los Angeles County Museum of Art (LACMA). He recovered a very valuable drawing by Michelangelo that someone with sticky fingers borrowed from the museum.

The Renaissance Master's Study of a Male Torso has an estimated value of about four million dollars. A wealthy collector recently offered the museum $3.2 million dollars for it, and they respectfully declined the kind offer.

The 16th Century 7x10" black charcoal sketch was on loan to the museum by an extremely wealthy Swiss collector and is among less than a handful of Michelangelo sketches in private hands in the whole world today.

While I was talking to Big Ray, he asked if I would accompany him on an assignment to Bel Air in the 90077. He felt four eyes would be better than just two.

Of course, I told him I would do it, and I also mentioned to him that I would need his help as well on a bank embezzlement case I was working on for a major bank downtown LA in the Bunker Hill Financial District.

He replied that he would be glad to assist in any way possible. I knew he would. He was a good friend, the best. He said he would call me in the next couple of days and set something up. I said, "Have your agent call my agent." That's how we do things in the 90077 zip code. Then he laughed.

While I was driving my beloved classic 1964 Chevy Impala 409 Super Sport down the 405 freeway and listening to the incomparable disc jockey, DJ Mr. Art Laboe, I heard that the famous California Grunion were running at Huntington Beach, Surf City, USA.

Do you recall the Beach Boys and Jan and Dean? That is where they used to hang out in the 1960s and 1970s as well as a lot of other very renowned singers and world-famous surfers.

The Grunions are wet, wild, and weird looking little fish that come ashore at night to spawn, usually from March through August of each year. A fishing license is required to catch them for people over 16 and there are no requirements for those 15 and under.

Only bare hands may be used to catch these cute little fishes. Their scientific name is Leuresthes Tenuis. Greenish-silver in color with blue stripes on the side and cheek. They are about 6" long and the females are a bit larger than the males. They live in the shallow ocean between Point Conception, California and Point Abreojos, Baja California, Mexico.

I love to go to the beach at night when the Grunion are running. The Grunion legend is as much a part of Southern California beach lore as sand pails, barbeques, body guards, and in the old days, long nose surf boards.

There are several musical odes to the Grunion, with most being titled The Grunion Run. The State Department Fish and Game website lists cooking tips for our little friends. For example: "Roll in flour and yellow corn mean, deep fry, and sprinkle with salt."

I never eat them, I just like to catch them. I went on my first Grunion run in the late 1960's. Boy that was a long time ago! I must be getting old. Even though they had been around for a long, long time, it wasn't until the 1940's that the fish sparked scientific interest, when Boyd W. Walker, a marine biologist at the famous Scripps Institute of Oceanography in La Jolla, California realized that the fishes' mating cycle was tied to the ocean tides.
Many years later, environmentalists pointed to the Grunion in debates about whether grooming sand may harm the beach eco system.

In a recent lawsuit, State officials against wealthy landowners in exquisite Malibu, who hire bulldozers to scoop sand from a public shore, said these actions disrupt the Grunion's natural spawning cycle.

The Grunion is named for the Spanish word for 'grunter'. After the highest tides are triggered by a new or full moon usually from March through August, the little fish's shimmy from the waves mainly on southland and northern Baja California beaches. Some have been seen as far north at San Francisco Bay.

The females bury their eggs under slick sand, which cradles them for about two weeks until the high tide shakes them open and washes the young Grunion to their home in the ocean. There is a whole other world under the sand that we know so little about.

The way the Grunion ritual unfolds is that the female dashes into the beach and drills herself into the shore with her head flailing above the sand as she discharges as many as 3,000 eggs.

Several males appear to envelop her and emit a kind of milk which fertilizes the eggs. The spawning takes only seconds. Then the male hustles back into the ocean, while the female pulls herself out of the sand and gladly follows him into the beautiful sea. It is a mating dance routine that hundreds, sometimes thousands, of Grunion perform every year.

When you try to catch them with your hands, which you must, they usually just hop out of your hand. They are fast little things.

Once I found out that the Grunion were running, I called one of my lady friends. I am getting older; however, I still have a lot of women who like me. I am not quite sure why, however, I am glad they do.

I do have a lovely wife now, lucky for me she has poor eyesight and thinks that I am good looking. After my ex-wife betrayed me, took all of my hard -earned life savings and deserted me after 33 years of caring and loving her, I was not sure if I will ever get married again.

Obviously, not all women are ungrateful and dishonorable like she was. But you have to be careful on those second marriages the marriage counselors say. And they should know, right? Anyway, I guess that is not unusual these days.

The woman I called is Tamara Shoemaker. She's in her forties, has lovely long black hair, big beautiful sparking green eyes, a very nice figure, and she is highly intelligent and owns her own business and is its CEO (Chief Executive Officer.)

And, she loves to dance and so do I. I am older now, bust can 'bust a move' when I have to. The only problem is that the next day I can hardly get out of bed, but please don't tell anyone I told you that or I will deny it completely.

I have never found anything in my life that is more romantic and exciting to me, and hopefully to my dates, than to go Grunion hunting at the beach about midnight with a lovely companion under the moon and the stars with t barbeque pit full of smoldering wood, hot dogs, hamburgers, marshmallows, and corn-on-the-cob. Yum, yum!

When I called Tamara, I told her I heard Mr. Art Laboe on the radio on 103.5 'Oldies but Goodies' station telling about the Grunion running tonight. She said she would love to see the Grunion Run; however, she didn't want to catch any because they are a little bit too slimy for her.

When I picked her up at her lovely home in Huntington Beach close to the water, she looked quite ravishing and charming. Of course, she usually does. She had on a tight, form-fitting (and she has a *nice* form) black bikini with crystal buttons, and over that a stunning black sweater with a hoodie to keep her head warm.

I felt I could do a pretty good job of keeping her head and her other body parts warm, though. We had just an absolutely delightful evening and I took her home about 5 am (0500 military time).

Tammy and the PI, I mused. Had kind of a nice ring to it, don't you think? A natural high at the beach. It just does not get any better!

I finally dragged my old body out of bed about noon after the simply perfect exceptional night at the beach chasing Grunion and Tamara.

I noticed Big Ray had left me a message. When I called him back, he made some wisecrack about my sleeping habits, but I just ignored him. I was just too tired to explain why I was up so late.

He said he was on his way over to my place in Hermosa Beach, not far from where he lived, and that we should grab some grub and head over to a home he wanted me to visit with him.

The home was in Bel Air, one of the most expensive private real estate communities in the US, and probably in the world. In the 90077 zip code, the homes sell now for $345,000, if you can even find one for that, and upwards of $72,000,000. Yes, that's seventy-two million dollars and up. The median price today is just under two million.

The house had 15 bedrooms, 15 bathrooms, with 23,000 square feet of living space. It had five kitchens, a Koi pond, and was surrounded by giant palm trees.

The palatial, extremely elegant estate was built by the King of Saudi Arabia, Abdullah bin Laden al Ziza in 1989. They tore down the existing home, which was also quite nice by the way. In its place, he built a French style mansion and a two-story guest house.

It lies on 2.38 acres, which is a large lot for this area. In 1992, the home was sold to a new owner who had it redesigned by a famous architect from North Hollywood, of all places. In the new reception area, a Baccarat crystal chandelier can be seen at every turn.

The dining room comfortably seats 50 guests. There's a theater with a floor to ceiling fireplace. The master suite alone is 4,000 square feet, larger than a lot of entire homes. The queen's spa and boutique have gold and silver vanities. The king's bathroom is done with jade, marble walls, and a stained-glass ceiling. The motor court holds twenty cars, and there's also a four-car garage.

Big Ray had received a discreet request from the home's new owner, Mr. Janos Ilinfrolovsky, a Russian, who stated that two extremely valuable paintings had been stolen from the home along with two pieces of jewelry that the former *Czar* of Russia, Nicholas II, had owned at one time.

He told Ray that he did not want to report the theft to the LAPD because he wanted no publicity. This secrecy is not unusual for some very rich people, however, when Ray checked Janos out, he learned he had been a Colonel in the former KGB, the Russian secret police.

No wonder he didn't want any publicity! I am sure there are lots of people in Russia and all over Europe and the former Soviet Union who would like to get their paws on him. I am not sure what they would do to him, but I can imagine it would not be pleasant.

When we finished our preliminary investigation and walk-through of the palatial estate, and we finished talking to the wealthy owner, the former KGB agent, Janos Ilinfrolovsky and his assistant and obvious bodyguard, Igor Prelinaya, I told Ray I was very hungry.

For some reason, I am always hungry. Ray said fine. We went to the famous *Brown Derby* restaurant at the corner of Hollywood and Vine.

Many famous Hollywood stars and rich people have eaten at the Derby over the last 50 years or so. I ordered a filet mignon with two New England lobster tails, a baked potato with sour cream, butter and cheese, garlic bread, and a Caesar salad. Just scrumptious, absolutely superb! The service was also exemplary, as usual.

Ray, being a healthy eater, ordered a grilled chicken breast, clam chowder, and white corn with mixed vegetables. Go figure. If I had that, I would be hungry again in about an hour.

As we were thoroughly enjoying our very expensive and simply scrumptious five-star meal, which Ray's client Janos was paying for by the way, I told Ray that I had recently discovered a list of the 25 Biggest Flops of Recent History. I asked him if he could name them. He got a few correct, but I got more. They were listed as:

1. Ford Edsel (1957-59).
   Faulty engineering and misguided marketing. Ford sold only 116,000 and lost $350 million. It was named after one of Henry Ford's sons. I rode in one in 1959 and I thought it was a great ride.

2. Smell-o-Vision. (1960)
   Technically the first and only film made in this format and it 'stank.'

3. Bell Rocket Belt (1960s)
   Flight time only 21 seconds.

4. Philadelphia Phillies (1964)
   Blew the NL Pennant after holding a 6 ½ game lead with 12 games left.

5. Moose Murders (1983)

6. Michele Phillips and Dennis Hopper (1970)
   They both had five spouses. She was a singer with the Mama's and Papa's and he was an actor in the Easy Rider movie. Their marriage lasted about 8 days.

7. Paper Clothing (1960's)
   Did not last.

8. Webvan.com (1999-2001)
   Online grocery delivery service lasted only 18 months. It was ahead of its time.

9. Susan B. Anthony One Dollar Coin (1979-81)
   Millions were not sold and never left the vault.

10. Percent Symbol % for Prince (1993-2000)
    Great singer, though.

11. Bay of Pigs (1961)
    1,440 invaded Cuba. 1,200 were captured by Fidel Castro's troops.

12. Premier, R. J. Reynolds Smokeless Cigarette (1988)

13. Rudy Juliani Campaign (2008)
    Spent $66 million and got zero votes.

14. WIN (1974)
    President Ford's weapon to fight inflation.

15. Carrie (1988)
    Broadway play, based on Stephen King's novel. Big flop.

16. New COKE (1985)
    A new formula flopped after 99 years of the classic Coke.

17. Chicago White Sox (1976)
    Played baseball in shorts. What were they thinking?

18. Comb-Over Hairstyle (1980s)
    It does not fool anyone; just looks odd.

19. XFL (2001)
    Lasted only one season.

20. DeLorean Cat (1981)
    Only made 9,000 cars, then went bankrupt.

21. Monkeys, Jim Hendrix Tour (1967)
    Hendrix left the tour due to the Monkey's younger fans.

22. Can't Stop the Music (1980)
    Village People movie with Olympic star, Bruce Jenner, on an award for the worst film of the year.

23. Jell-O for Salads (1980s)
    Gelatin for salads. The idea and taste just did not go over with consumers.

24. Psychic Espionage Research (1970-1995)
    US learned nothing new.

25. Sony Beta-Max (1980s)
    First video player on the market, but was outmaneuvered by VHS format.

Naming these flops with Big Ray over lunch was kind of like playing Jeopardy or some other word game. Fun! I could probably name 25 flops in my own personal life over the same period of years, but I didn't wish to do that! Too depressing. Maybe someday I will write a book to list them for posterity. Then again, maybe not!

After a delightful dinner, and some great conversation with my friend and partner, Big Ray, we walked out to Ray's new car. It was a BMW 5 Series 'Gran Turismo'. It has a 4.4 liter, 400 hp advanced hydrogen V-8 Turbo powered engine.
It is built almost like an expensive Swiss watch or a Rolex. It has an 8-speed automatic transmission and 20" run-flat tires, with the optional $7,000-star shaped chrome wheels, I-drive, and full-time all-wheel drive.

And, the cabin boasts exquisite custom fine fitted leather upholstery with unsurpassed hand polished red burl walnut interior trim. BMW inarguably is one of the finest road production vehicles in the whole world. And it has been so for over 60 years now.

Just as I was about to get in the passenger's comfortable seat, I felt a rush of air go rapidly past my head. Then two seconds later, I heard a little swishing sound that I recognized. I had heard that same awful noise before, unfortunately.
I knew instinctively that it was a bullet from a silenced sniper rifle. I think they missed me because I had just started to bend over to get into the car. If they had shot at me a little bit sooner, I would have been DOA—dead on arrival to the *morgue*!

Ray looked very worried about me, naturally, and asked if I were alright. I said it was nothing, that I was fine. I was, however, indeed worried. But I didn't want him to think I was a wuss.

People die every day. I know that. There's car crashes, cancer, lightning, floods, hurricanes, tornadoes, earthquakes, tsunamis, and even stray bullets from some knucklehead gang members trying to 'make their bones' with the 'shot caller' in their gang.

"What's the difference how you die, I thought to myself." Although, I did not express that aloud to my friend, Ray.

We pulled out our weapons in a few seconds after the incident. I pulled my trusty .357 Smith and Wesson Magnum 6" barrel revolver from my shoulder holster. And Ray had his big Colt model 1911 .45 caliber automatic pistol. His was way too much gun for me, but he was 6'9" and 250 pounds, you may recall. I am 6' even and 199 pounds on a good day.

We walked very carefully over to the back of the parking lot next to an old warehouse where there were some trash cans. That's where we thought the shot came from. There was 'no one home', but they did leave us a little present.

They had split without taking their apparent weapon of choice. It was a Russian made Snayperskayaova sniper rifle. It was a very unusual looking gun.

It had a large cut out in its stock to make it lighter, and a pistol grip that allowed you to wrap your hand completely around it. A soft rubber cheek piece was glued to the top of the stock and a rubber eye piece on the very detailed scope.

The rifle was semi-automatic and fired 7.62 rounds, which is what the NATA forces use around the world. The lengthy action and slender 22" barrel with attached muzzle, made this Russian sniper rifle a long and elegant weapon.

The cut-out stock helped keep it fairly light for what is usually a very heavy sniper rifle. We took the exotic looking rifle with us to run finger prints on it at the LAPD. We knew LAPD's forensic lab—brand new and state-of-the-art—would probably not find any prints. The sniper likely wore gloves and was probably a pro, judging from the type of weapon.

The Russian made Snayperskayaova rifle was quite something, and had cost somebody a lot of rubles—Russian money. Now all we had to figure out was *who.*

I returned the next day to my office still thinking about Ray's case of the stolen and very valuable items. And, of course, who might have taken the shot at this old PI. Not a very nice thing to do, I thought anyway.

My office, as I have mentioned, is on Wilshire Boulevard, between downtown LA and the famous Miracle Mile. For decades, this has been a center of business commerce with buildings occupied by some business powerhouses like very large banks, Texaco, IBM, and the Getty Oil Company.
Recently, there have been built a lot of mid-rise condominiums and upscale luxury apartment buildings along Wilshire.

My office is located in the Traveler's Insurance Building at Wilshire and La Brea, in the 12th story, top floor.

Developers are building a 482-unit luxury apartment with a retail complex just across the street. Some of the locals are upset that they are tearing down the famous old Columbia Savings and Loan building. It was built around the 1960's with what was then very modernist architecturally significant design.

Still today, it is a very attractive structure. The Columbia Savings and Loan Building opened in 1965. Wilshire Boulevard has always been considered a transit boulevard with rapid transit bus lines and Metro train stops. It is one of the few places in the city where high rises are allowed, except in downtown LA.

Believe it or not, I was born close to my classy Wilshire Boulevard office on Fedora Street, close to Olympic and Alvarado, just south of Wilshire. The property lot had two houses on it, and I was born in the smaller one in the back.

I was not actually born in the house, of course. I just lived there for a short time, after my birth at the grand old California Medical Center, located at the intersection of the 110 Harbor and the 10 Santa Monica Freeways, right downtown LA.

The houses were owned by a very nice Japanese family, loyal to America and hard working. But they were unjustly, unfairly moved to *Manzanar* Internment Camp close to Lone Pine, California, off Highway 395, heading toward Bishop, the Mammoth Lakes, and Reno, Nevada.

The city rented the houses out until the poorly treated Japanese family was able to return to their own home after the end of World War II.

Very close to my office on Wilshire Boulevard was where the formerly unsurpassed and world-renowned Ambassador Hotel and Coconut Grove Restaurant was located for many years.

It was torn down in more recent years and the City of LA built a beautiful new high school, a middle school, and an elementary school, as well as some very nice additional structures on the very large site.

Many of the famous and wealthy people of Hollywood during the flamboyant era of the burgeoning movie business of the era from the 1930's – 1960's stayed in the fabulous hotel suites, entertained in the incomparable Coconut Grove, and/or had rendezvous with some starlets or 'wannabe' actresses there.

Also close to my office, was the old Rampart Division building of the LAPD, at 3rd and Union Streets, in what is called the Westlake business district business area of LA, just north of Wilshire Boulevard and west of the 110 Harbor Freeway.

It is deserted now, but that building was where I worked for many years when I was a detective in the Robbery and Homicide Division with the LAPD.

One concern I have in considering buying my old work place, is that tenant rents are fairly low in this area currently.

And, if I did find tenants, I would have to spend a considerable amount of money to turn the police type station into an ordinary office building. The owner says that the one-way glass windows come at no extra charge!

Funny, I thought. After some detailed discussions with my personal real estate broker, my CPA, (Certified Public Accountant), and my real estate attorney, I decided to pass on purchasing my old homestead.

While I was at my office, I started to track the missing valuables from Ray's client Janos' mansion. One of the missing paintings was by Claude Monet, the French artist. It was called *The Walkers, Bazille and Camille*, and was worth about $20 million dollars.

The other painting taken was by Edgar Degas, also a French Impressionist painter. His beauty was titled, *Dancer with a Tambourine,* valued at maybe $15 million dollars.

I will have to call a good friend of mine who works at Christie's Auction House in LA, to get a better idea of just exactly how much money we are talking about between the two exquisite and rare paintings.

In addition, one piece of the *Czar's* missing jewelry was an ideal brilliant cut V.VS-2 clarity G graded exquisite 10 carat diamond ring. No telling how much it would be worth, and it is probably priceless due to its heritage. I would guess its worth at $2 million dollars or more.

And the other missing piece was a magnificent total 50 carat weight diamond, ruby, and emerald necklace. The gorgeous item was of absolutely superb quality, as to be expected. And, ideally brilliantly cut like the other ring. Once again, I am sure priceless, but to assign a value I would guess $5 million dollars.

I will ask my friend at Christie's Auction House about these two pieces when I talk to her about the two lovely missing paintings.

PROFESSOR ALAN DALE DICKINSON

I made some confidential, encrypted phone calls for my big buddy, Ray the PI. I called a friend I have at Interpol in the Paris regional office. I wanted to check out our Russian friends, Ray's new clients, Janos Ilinfrolovsky and his number one body guard, Igor Prelinaya.

Ray did not have nearly as many contacts in LA, or outside the city, as I do. He was not a retired police detective, like me. In my prior profession, I made a great deal of valuable contacts both inside and outside law enforcement, throughout the US and abroad. Interpol, MI-5, and the New Scotland Yard, to name a few.

When my friend at Interpol called me back after he did a lot of secret investigative work for me, he told me that indeed Janos was a former high-ranking agent in the KGB. He had a large private office in the Kremlin building just off Red Square.

He allegedly had stolen several very valuable paintings and several other items including the two missing paintings, ring, and necklace. He had taken advantage of his prestigious position at the Soviet Secret Police.

Janos had supposedly amassed a fortune of about $5 billion US dollars over a 20-year period before he left Mother Russia for Bel Air in Southern California, USA.

My friend also told me that Janos was no neophyte to embezzlement, coercion, intimidation, threats of bodily harm, torture, theft, and making people 'disappear', just to name a few. He was quite obviously not a warm and fuzzy man, to say the least.

He was said to have nerves of steel and ice water in his veins. Janos' eyes were reported to be very dark, cold, shadowy, and dangerous.

His voice had a low, snarling growl to it. I observed these things first hand when Ray and I met him at his mansion. He was known at the KGB as a "terminator", like the character played by Arnold Schwarzenegger, because of the many people he personally made disappear.

A former agent and employee of his at the KGB was quoted as saying, "A meeting with Janos when he is upset with you over something, is an encounter of the worst kind. The only thing worse is death." Kind of tells you something about the man, doesn't it?

When my Interpol friend finished telling me what he had found out about Janos, he went on to say that as bad as Janos is, and that is very, very bad, Janos is a saint compared to his number one body guard, Igor Prelinaya.

Igor is a stone-cold killer from the icy region of Siberia, Russia. And he is pure ice himself. He had no remorse for taking out his enemies, targets, and even sometimes so-called friends for that matter.

PROFESSOR ALAN DALE DICKINSON

Even though he always carried two matching chrome plated 9mm Barretta automatic shoulder holsters and a .38 caliber revolver on his ankle, he really didn't need a gun. His body was an efficient, highly trained, lethal weapon.

He had a black belt in Karate, among several other martial arts disciplines. I remember thinking to myself, when I met him at Janos' mansion, the malevolent light in his very dark, deep eyes sparked with pure evil.

The man is indeed a devil. He is definitely a ticking time bomb with a lit fuse just waiting to go off. I just hoped that Ray and I were not around when Igor explodes.

I was still in my office and I was still wondering what ilk had tried to put my lights out when they took a shot at me. I knew it wasn't Igor, nor one of Janos' other big, square built, gun toting henchmen.

They all wanted me to retrieve the missing paintings and jewelry. So, they clearly would not want me DOA—dead on arrival. And they were from Russia, not LA, and would not know where to even begin to look for their stolen items.

I didn't think this was connected with my IBBC bank embezzlement investigation, however, you never know for sure about these things. While I was pondering the shooting and my almost shortened life span, I called another friend of mine.

In my line of work, you cannot survive without a lot of good, trustworthy friends and associates. I called the Deputy Chief of

Police for the LAPD, Jim *Jimbo* Bowen. His office was in the brand-new state-of-the-art police headquarters located by City Hall at 1st and Spring Streets in LA.

I told him we should get together to play golf or walk our dogs together soon, and that I needed a big favor. I said that I was looking for two extremely valuable paintings, a Money and a Degas. And, also a historically rare ring and necklace.

I asked him to check with the pawn shops that possibly handle high end stolen items like these. They I asked that he also check with any second story burglars in town who might have done this little piece of work, or who may know someone who did.

Finally, I asked him to keep his ear to the ground for any information related to the case that might be of interest to me or help me locate the missing valuables.

While my friend Jimbo at the LAPD was discreetly checking out all the usual suspects for me, I drove around LA myself contacting all my CI's (confidential informants) just to see what information I could shake loose.

On the third day of my ferreting around and beating the bushes, I got a classified and untraceable cell phone call from the deputy chief. He told me, "Off the record Charlie, go see a man named Little Louie Cantanilli at a jewelry store located on Pico Boulevard close to Alvarado Street downtown LA near Korea Town." And he added, "Tell Louie that Jimbo sent you."

When I got to the store, I noticed it was not very nice on the outside. But the inside was full of rare and costly jewelry items and a few expensive paintings.

He was expecting me, thanks to Jimbo. He told me, "Confidentially, a Frenchman with an obvious alias of *Henri Jean Renoir,* was making the rounds in LA's fencing business and trying to sell the subject two paintings and jewelry for a total of $10 million."

Very cheap, I would say. But "Henri" had to make a quick sale and make a clean get away ASAP. Luckily, he had left his address and cell number with *Little Louie* in case Cantanilli decided he wanted to buy the items.

I had heard that Louie was connected to the mob back east in Chicago. But who knows or even cares these days, with all the other problems the US is facing, I thought to myself.

Little Louie said that Henri, or whatever the guy's real name is, would be staying at the Bonaventure Hotel on Figueroa Street, downtown LA just off the 110 Harbor Freeway.

He said he would only be in town for a week. After that, he'd told Louie, he was returning to France via Canada. No doubt on a forged passport, I thought.

I paid Cantanilli a finder's fee for his golden information. I would probably have missed Henri by a few days had it not been for Louie's much needed assistance.

I reminded Louie when I left him not to tell Henri that anyone had been looking for him, if he happened to call or come back in. Louie said he would have done that for me anyway, since I was a friend of the Deputy Chief at the LAPD.

I made a quick call to Big Ray who was thrilled with the good news on his case. He said he would meet me at the Bonaventure Hotel in 15 minutes. We rode up the all glass elevator that hung on the outside of the hotel building, to the 25th floor. Nice view of LA's skyline, I thought.

I had been to the Bonaventure many times over the years. The first time was in 1988. It has a lot of nice shops, some exquisite restaurants, as well as a lot of wonderful hotel suites.

We located Henri's Room 2525 and lucky for us he answered the door, thinking we were room service which he had apparently just ordered—some expensive French cuisine for lunch no doubt.

Henri was very surprised when he opened the door to find us instead of the delicious food. He looked a bit intimidated, as Big Ray stands looming there at 6'9". And it was clear that Big Ray and I were both carrying heat.

Henri admitted that he had indeed done the job. He was quite proud of it apparently. Crooks have very big egos, as I have found out over the many years of working with them. I made Henri a fair offer, at least I thought it was fair.

I said I would give him $150,000 via wire transfer EFT to his bank in France for the return of the two paintings, ring, and necklace. No questions asked. And, I would need his promise he would never come back to LA on business again.

If he did not accept, I told him, I would turn him over immediately to the Deputy Chief of the LAPD, and he would spend the next 10-15 years in prison doing hard time with Americans. And you know how much some French people hate Americans.

He decided to play call after only 60 seconds, just as I expected him to do. He told Ray and me where he had placed the valuables. They were locked in the hotel's large safekeeping vault reserved for their wealthier guests. He quickly retrieved them for us.

I gave Henri the secret EFT confirmation number to collect on the wire transfer funds. Within two hours, Henri (or whatever his real name was) was on a Boeing 747 Jumbo Jet leaving LAX airport for Vancouver, British Columbia, Canada.

Shortly thereafter, Big Ray and I returned the exceptionally valuable items to Janos Ilinfrolovsky at his huge mansion in Bel Air. Ray charged him $100,000. That's $50,000 for me and $50,000 for himself. A generous split, I thought.

Janos gave Ray a cashier's check, adding the additional $150,000 Ray had paid out to Henri the thief for a total of $250,000. A quarter million dollars, just like it was peanuts to him.

That's just how rich he apparently was. And it was a small amount to pay for the return of $40-$50 million dollars' worth of valuables, wouldn't you agree?

But Ray and I decided that we would check out clients more carefully in the future. Neither of us liked working with, nor being associated with, alleged criminals like Janos and Igor.

I thanked him for the generous split on the fee. He said that it was only fair and that he would not have been able to recover the items without my assistance and contacts.

That was true, however, he could have given me less and I would have been just as happy to have helped him out. He is a good friend and he has assisted me in the past with insurance fraud cases which is his area of expertise.

Now, I really needed to do some more research and get back to the job of my IBBC bank case. I had checked in with Jerry, the bank Executive Vice President, several times during the past week while assisting Big Ray.

I had gotten updates from him and also had him do some research for me on confidential bank records related to the embezzlement of the $75 million dollars.

I thought again how the $50,000 fee Big Ray had given me was some serious and easy green (money). And I would like to return the favor sometime in the future.

Chapter Four

Like a Needle in a Hay Stack

A DETECTIVE'S WORK never ends. I had wanted to go to San Diego, California, right after I returned from Mother Russia, after my encounter of the worst kind with Viktor Kharchenko, *The Fisherman,* but I was not prepared at that time. I needed some rest and further research to resume the IBBC embezzlement case investigation.

I was way too exhausted, and frozen from the Siberian cold and snow, to function properly mentally.

As I pointed out previously, Viktor is a stone-cold killer. He has not one iota of remorse for his enemies or targets. One of these days, though, perhaps his flow of money will stop, and then what?

Looking for suspects or perpetrators is like looking for a needle in a hay stack. Some of the IBBC bank executives who were somewhat suspect after my initial probe into the seventy-five-million-dollar embezzlement scheme included the following:

Bruce *'The Eye'* Englebert—not the singer, but a senior VP. And William R. *'Smitty'* Smith, the San Diego Regional President—not the president over the whole bank, just the San Diego area. The overall President of IBBC had an office in London, England, Great Britain, with a satellite office suite in LA.

There were a few other tasty suspects I thought of, however, most of them did not have the confidential access codes to that large an amount of the green stuff (money).

Someone with a lot of juice and power had to get the funds transferred from the bank's central cash vault in the basement to the main office building at 333 S. Hope Street, downtown LA and on to the San Diego Regional Headquarters cash vault.

Of course, they did not move the money via Brinks Armored Transport. Actually, very little cash is moved that way now. This is due to the fact that numerous Southern California armored vehicles are held up each year. LA has become the bank robbery capital of the world.

Most all big-ticket transactions are handled by EFT electronic funds transfers that wire funds over secure and encrypted phone lines or secret satellite link-ups. Once in San Diego, the perpetrator 'perp' or thief, would have to get the funds into a more liquid and fluent form and get it ready to move to Russia with a few little stops in between.

They had to do all of this without coming to the attention of the internal bank examiners. And they do not miss very much, believe me. And the perps would have to escape notice by the

FDIC, the Feds, or national bank examiners from Washington, D.C. as well. All of these very diligent entities might notice the extremely large and somewhat suspicious cash transaction in the EFT.

Here is a brief history of my primary suspects:

Mr. Bruce 'The Eye' Englebert, Senior VP. He has a reputation for being a ladies' man, even though he has been married for years. His wife is related to a former Board of Directors member at the bank's Los Angeles US headquarters.

The bank's world headquarters was moved to London, England, where the global bank President and the international Chairman of the Board (COB) now hold court.

Bruce and his family also owned a lot of the bank's preferred stock. Senior bank managers just put up with him, but they really want to zap, fire him for his lack of business ethics. In the 1980's – 1990's, he allegedly smoked a lot of pot—marijuana, Mary Jane, weed, puff, smoke, junk, Jamaica Red, etc.—and also did a lot of cocaine. They used to say back in the day, "There's no pain with cocaine!" Boy, were they wrong about that one!

Bruce is supposedly clean—drug free—now, but he still drinks like a fish. Or so I have been informed. He makes a very good and viable suspect in the embezzlement and theft of all that money—moolah, cabbage, green.

Mr. George Claremont Moore, Executive VP. He is originally from the San Bernardino, Riverside area. That's the so-called Inland Empire (IE), as Southern Californians refer to it. I am not sure exactly why. It is an area just straight east about 50 miles from LA.

It is way too hot out there in the IE for me, and it's getting overcrowded and smoggy. Bob Hope the famous comedian joked about being way out there in Cucamonga. Out in the boonies, he said.

He went through the Inland Empire often on his way from Hollywood to Las Vegas, Nevada. There, he entertained with the Rat Pack, which included the *Chairman of the Board*, Frank Sinatra, the very funny and talented Sammy Davis Jr., and Peter Lawford who married a Kennedy sister. Her father was Joe Kennedy and her brother President JFK.

Also, in the Rat Pack were Dean *Dino* Martin, the well-known singer and actor who felt that he was never very talented at all. And, also the lesser known Rat Pack member was comedian, Joey Bishop.

Back then, Cucamonga was just a desert with a lot of vineyards. Today only a few of the wineries remain and it has become a very large and wealthy city (Rancho Cucamonga). It's located off the 15 and the 10 Freeways, heading to the steep Cajon Pass in the San Bernardino Mountains.

Over the pass and on the back side of the mountains lies Victorville, California. Roy Rogers, the famous TV Cowboy and his wife, Dale Evans, lived there for many years after he decided to get out of the Hollywood media circus and away from all the paparazzi.

They and their large family built a very nice memory-filled Cowboy Museum, which is still located there today.

George with the IBBC bank, however, lives in the high rent district now, instead of the hot Inland Empire desert. He and his family live in Brentwood, California, just a block away from Bel Air and Beverly Hills.
He's near the famous Rodeo Drive shopping district. It's part of LA County, but you would think you are in a different state!

He flies to San Diego when necessary, by helicopter. He sometimes uses an extra IBBC bank office downtown LA for work, to save on the commute to San Diego. The chopper is located on the heliport on the roofs of the bank's buildings. Just one of his many executive benefits.

George graduated from the well-known prestigious Claremont College University system located in Claremont, California just off the 10 Freeway. It is quite a lovely community and a world class University.

George invested a huge amount of money with the infamous Bernard L. *Bernie* Madoff in New York City, New York. Bernie had some security brokers, or front men, working for him in Beverly Hills in the LA area. George and his family lost every penny they had during the horrific and tragic 2007-2010 economic global financial catastrophe and worldwide financial meltdown.

Mr. Robert *'Smitty'* Smith, the San Diego Area IBBC Bank VP.

He and his family live in a high-rise townhouse in downtown San Diego, which has a commanding magnificent view of the lovely boat harbor, as well as of the eternally beautiful Coronado Island. For many years, Coronado was a huge US Navy base for the Pacific Theater.

It is little used by the Navy anymore, and now there are a lot of million dollar plus homes located on the waterfront.

Smitty, just like thousands of other people including VP Mr. Moore above, lost an entire life savings when the stock market died of a sudden heart attack in 2007. He also saw his IBBC bank employee 401k payroll savings plan, with his over five million dollars in it, tank in 2008.

He also tragically lost his vacation homes located in Cannes, France, a waterfront mansion in Miami, Florida on Key West Island, and an absolutely majestic old castle on Lake Como in Italy. I have been to that lake and took a boat cruise that toured the city in 1996 when I spent a month covering the whole country of Italy.

I stopped for two or three days in each of the magnificent Italian cities—Roma, Venice, Tuscany, Naples, the scenic little island of Capri, the ancient city of Pompeii, among others. Lake Como is clearly an incredible and remarkable place to visit.

I understand George Clooney, Tom and Katie Cruise, and many other wealthy and famous people from the US and throughout Europe are reportedly owners of some of the castles found there.

I was told that during World War II—the big one—the Allied Command used several of the beautiful old homes and castles for their headquarters. Prior to that, the German and Italian Generals had done the same.

Now, I said to myself, "Charlie—and I have been talking to myself a lot lately and I hope it is not an early sign of senility setting in— "How did they get the funds to San Diego? How did they get the money from the San Diego branch to their own offshore bank accounts?

How did they move that much green stuff to Moscow, Russia? And how did they move the money again to *The Fisherman's* bank in Omsk, Siberia, Russia?

I set up my cover story with Mr. Frankhoffer *The Jackal* Executive Vice President and with the bank's Board of Directors at the IBBC bank in LA. They told the senior management, as well as several key employees, that I was doing research for a movie the bank was going to bankroll.

The bank was well-known for its glitz and glamour division that lent a large sum of money to the major Hollywood Studios, Paramount, Sony, Universal, MGM, and Touchstone, just to name a few. Most of the studios were located in LA, Hollywood, Burbank, or the San Fernando Valley.

The bank's staff was told to give me unrestricted access to the internal workings of their larger cash flow movements, etc. They seemed to buy my cover story when I got to the bank.

I didn't notice any tails, nor any bugs (listening devices) in my temporary office they gave me on the 20th Floor. I swept the room twice for any little 'friends. I didn't find any so I assumed that I was not being spied on—at least for now.

Oh, by the way, I wanted to let you know when I was in Russia, I heard some very interesting rumors about the IBBC bank. I was told by some very reliable sources, "The bank is selling weapons to small foreign countries."

"And they hold very large deposits for some unsavory Columbian and Mexican Drug Cartel kingpins—money laundering as it were—for a fee of 10%, to 20% of the account balances."

These illegal deals transfer some of the bank's general funds into numbered Swiss bank accounts for the top executives just in case they have to run for the hills from the FBI or Feds or should the bank be shut down by the FDIC due to millions of dollars' worth of bad debt and very toxic real estate loans, residential, commercial, and industrial.

I will certainly have to investigate these allegations when I have some time. And if I find out that there is any merit to any of the charges, I will report them to the FDIC, The Federal Reserve System, Department of Justice (DOJ), Department of Defense (DOD), Interpol in Europe, the FBI, and possibly also the CIA.

My eyes were getting a little bit tired and blurry from looking at all those numbers and the large number of zeroes, millions and billions, from the bank's wire transfer computer print outs, confidential logs, and instant messages.

So, I decided to take a break from my investigation, clear my head, and take a walk on the strand down by the San Diego Pier.

No, it was not to check out the very pretty women in their bikinis and bright but brief summer attire—well maybe just a little look or two wouldn't hurt me. San Diego has a lot of very attractive, friendly ladies, and is well known around the world for that material fact.

The strand is close to Old Town, which is a very lovely and cordial area full of gift shops with nautical themes and wonderful seafood restaurants. Some of them are quite famous. They have great lobster, and I just love lobster so I decided to sample some.

I felt like I deserved it after all my hard work on this case. The lobster was absolutely delicious at the Lobster World Bar and Grill where I ate and looked out over the grandiose and magnificent Pacific Ocean, one of the nicest seas on the planet.

All of a sudden, I felt a sharp pain in my right shoulder. It was almost like a red-hot poker or knife had been stuck into my flesh. Then I heard a little swishing noise which I recognized as a Remington sniper rifle shot.

I had been bending over to dust some sand off my pants when I was hit, otherwise I would have been in heaven sooner than expected with a kill shot to the head.

Obviously, someone found out I am investigating the seventy-five-million-dollar embezzlement from the IBBC bank.

I made a quick trip to the hospital emergency room and thanked God I was still alive and breathing. The ER has to report all gunshot wounds to the local police.

When the San Diego Police Department called me in for questioning, I asked them to call an old friend of mine at the LAPD, Big Jim Bowen, Deputy Chief in the Robbery and Homicide Unit. He is a good man with 30 years of placing his life on the line daily.

Jim immediately cleared up my little predicament with the locals. It only took a few stitches, as the .23 caliber bullet had gone straight through my shoulder and had not hit anything important—like my heart or brain.

I went back to my five-star hotel, the San Diego Bay Hilton on the Pacific, which had superb room service and gourmet food. Then I took a much-needed nap and I wanted to rest due to my wound. I was just a touch tired and weak from the ordeal, however, not too bad for an old guy.

I had been wounded while working a few times at the LAPD in downtown LA. So, it was not a new experience. Of course, you never get used to being shot or having a bad guy try to turn your lights out, but you do become accustomed to a certain amount of pain.

The next day, I went back to my temporary office at the IBBC bank building on the 20th Floor. From the window in my nice office, on a clear day you can see forever.

And in San Diego, it is clear almost 365 days a year. Just a bit of low hanging fog in the winter. It has some of the most comfortable and body pleasing and pleasant climates in the whole wide world—it truly does.

My wound was healing and I was feeling a lot better, thanks to the terrific ER doctor on duty that eventful day. Thank goodness I drew him and not some hack who had been up for 72 hours and taking Propofol.

I've mentioned the phrase many dancers use, "I'm going to bring it and I'm going to leave it all out on the dance floor". Detectives and private investigators, both public police officers and private detectives, do pretty much the same thing.

The only difference is that sometimes, just every once in a while, they have to leave their blood and guts, or sometimes their lives, on the 'dance floor'.

I called an old friend of mine named Carrie Summers. She lives in La Jolla, California, which is really close to San Diego.

It's a very affluent and upscale neighborhood and sits right on the gorgeous Pacific Ocean. It is also home to the Scripts Medical and Research Center. It is a private hospital and clinic and is one of the best in the whole world.
People come from all over the continent and globe to get tested and to receive treatment for several types of illnesses and diseases.

A lot of the major banks send their key executives there once a year for compete intensive physicals. It costs a great deal of money and it is considered to be a large fringe benefit, non-taxed, of course, for the bank officers.

The IBBC bank, my current case, sends its key executives to Scripts every year. They write it off as an expense naturally.

La Jolla is just absolutely lovely and so is my friend. Believe it or not she is a PI just like me. I worked with her at the LAPD *Rampart* Division close to MacArthur Park many years ago. She was an excellent detective and solved several high-profile crimes and difficult cases.

It was very difficult for her back in the day, because she was one of the few women police detectives, or even police officers, on the force. She got more than her fair share of teasing and razing, believe me.

I was always very impressed with the way she handled all the distractions and yet she somehow always got along with all the guys in the unit, as well as the male police officers on the mean streets of LA. Probably this was due to the fact that she is a *smart* and also a very strong and competent police detective, and she worked out a lot.

She also holds a Doctorate of Justice (DOJ) law degree with a specialty in Criminal Justice from a prestigious law school located in the quaint and lovely small community of Orange, California. Orange is located in Orange County, which some locals call *God's Country*.

Of course, this might be said about the whole US. If you have ever been to Orange, you will know what they mean and why they say that.

In Southern California, Orange County is referred to as the OC. There was a TV series based on this locale at one time. The show was not very good, as I recall. Orange is also not far from the well-known campus of the University of California at Irvine (UCI).

This college was built on land once owned by the famous and wealthy Mrs. Joan Irvine. She owned the thousands of acres of land formerly known as the Irvine Rancho. It had been in her family since the turn of the 19th Century.

She used to live in the fabulous Laguna Beach Art Colony in the 1970's and 1980's. She grew up in the lovely little beach enclave of Corona Del Mar, California.

Carrie still carries heat—a .357 Smith and Wesson Magnum revolver with a 3" barrel and loaded with either magnum rounds or a .38 caliber special +P bullets. It is a very easy to use weapon, light, and fits into her purse.

She also carries a lightweight 10 oz. Colt Cobra .38 caliber LT model revolver. It has 6 shots like most revolvers and she puts that one on her ankle when she wears slacks, and on her waist under her blouse when she wears a skirt or one of her lovely business suits.

She prefers pin striped suits with a bright red top. She also keeps a Taurus model 856 .38 caliber revolver with a 2" barrel 6 shot lightweight attn13.2 oz. which she stashes under her dashboard in her new Ford SHO automobile. You never know when it is going to 'rain'—get shot at—or when you might need an extra persuader. She always said that.

I was told by a good mutual friend of hers and mine that she had a .40 caliber unnamed automatic pistol once that jammed on her during a shoot-out in the Dog Town area of LA and she almost got killed. That explains why she never carries automatics any longer.

She can handle heavier fire power if she has to, like the police issue M-15 automatic rifle machine gun, or a police car repeater shot gun, or even the ever-popular street weapon of choice, the AK-47 assault machine guns, among other larger weapons whenever and wherever required.

Carrie is divorced and has three kids—young people who I am sure must drive her crazy even though they are great kids. She is active on various cruises and in civic circles.

She is the real deal and she is also quite a pistol, as the old saying goes. She has outward and inward beauty, brains, inner strength, and physical strength. She is 5'11" tall.

The reason I called Carrie was to say hello because I do not get to see her very often these days. We are both very busy with our PI businesses. I needed to ask her assistance on my IBBC bank embezzlement case I am currently working on.

She is an expert on bank wire transfers as well as how the drug cartels, their leaders, and various other white-collar criminals move their rubles (money) around the globe without getting caught a lot of the time unfortunately.

The promise of America to the international crooks, in their opinion anyway, is the access to a lot of easy money. Whether they actually see any of it from their evil, unethical, and criminal efforts and ill-gotten gains was something that will remain to be seen.

I did not tell Carrie that I had been shot, as I did not want her to worry about me. I had shaken my tail when I left my office, so I was not worried about her being in any kind of danger. Plus, she could always handle herself if anything went down.

I gave her some research material and important confidential bank documents and told her to call me when she was finished examining them. It would take a while since there was quite a lot of bank material.

After my nice visit with my old pal, I drove back down the 5 Freeway to San Diego. I have always loved San Diego all my life. I was born and raised in Southern California.

Los Angeles will always be my town. I was born and will, one day, die in LA—the wonderful City of Angels. There is an old movie entitled, "To Live and Die in LA". I do not recall the story, just the great title.

I got off the 5 Freeway which dead ends at the California-Mexican border in Tijuana. It is a terrific little, or not so little, community these days with wonderful shops and restaurants which have exquisite Mexican food with very good service.

I could tell that my office was now bugged as soon as I walked into the room where I had set up some hard-to-observe surveillance equipment of my own before I left town the other day.

Also, I noticed that I had picked up a tail again when I left my cozy and very classy Hilton Hotel this morning. I had ditched this tail in downtown San Diego before getting on the Freeway to go visit my friend and associate. Now the 'tail' is back.

Chapter Five
Follow the Money

THE FEDERAL RESERVE system or Fed, the Securities and Exchange Commission (SEC), the Manhattan District Attorney prosecutors, the New York State Attorney General in Albany, New York, the US Attorney General in Washington, D.C., the Internal Revenue Service (IRS), the Federal Deposit Insurance Corporation (FDIC), the New York Stock Exchange (NYSE).

The National Association of Security Exchange Dealers (NASDAQ) the US Postal Service (USPS), and many other agencies and organizations all spent months, even years, trying to follow the money that Bernie Madoff, his wife and sons, plus a few highly placed insiders, stole from his clients.

Many of these clients were wonderful and generous charities. Madoff grabbed with his greedy little hands approximately 65 billion dollars ($65,000,000,000). I am here to tell you that is a lot of zeroes folks! Old Bernie thought he got away with his scheme and refused to talk to the authorities.

Now we are going to follow the money to see where it will lead us in the very complicated and intriguing mystery that I find myself in the middle of at IBBC bank.

I think, and Carrie my friend and fellow PI, agrees that we have found possibly a very important clue in the IBBC bank case. An amount of approximately seventy-five million dollars was moved as follows:

a) From the bank's LA headquarters to
b) The bank's San Diego Regional Office, then
c) Forty million to the Bank of the Cayman Islands in the Caribbean
d) The other thirty-five million sent to a numbered Swiss bank account at the Credit Swiss Bank in Switzerland
e) A grand total of seventy-five million dollars was moved to the Soviet Kremlin National Bank and Trust Corporation (SKNBTC) located in Moscow, Russia.

Boy, after all that cabbage (money) swirling around the globe, and with all of those banks, I now have an enormous headache. Finally, as if that were not enough money travels, a large sum of cash was filtered through some nebulous backdoor channels to Russian Association of Farmers and Merchants Bank (RAFMB) in the city of Omsk, I believe.

The Soviet Kremlin Bank (SKNBTC) in Moscow, I am informed, is controlled by the Federal Security Service of the Russian Federation (FSB), which is the reincarnation of the KGB. This fact is not known by the general public, of course.

The bank's Chairman of the Board (COB) and Chief Executive Officer (CEO) is Vladimir Aleksyeyevich. He was formerly a very influential and high-ranking intelligence operative chief in the former Soviet Union.

Before the wall came crashing down, however, he and many other KGB officials quickly moved into other more profitable positions.

If you check to see who's running most of the free businesses in Russia today, you will discover that a great deal of them are owned and/or operated by former high-level KGB officers. Same old faces in new jobs. And many with new names—aliases.

In an effort to understand more clearly the IBBC bank's complicated financial transactions, and so to speak 'follow the money', as thoroughly as possible, I needed to do research first.

While discerning public banking in general, and with much more insight, I decided to do some in-depth research of the FED, both in the US and in Russia.

The following information is relevant and important to the case, and confidential. It is not known by many people outside the banking industry. This financial information may very well assist anyone with their personal financial or bank dealings, especially in troubling, confusing, and volatile times.

The Federal Reserve System:

What is the Fed?
The nation's money manager. Unlike other major nations where strong central banks were the rule, the US throughout the 19th Century relied on a patchwork banking system that in

effect left the nation's economic welfare just up to chance. And the nation has paid a price for that errant policy more than once over the years since then.

Not that there were no precedents for a central bank in US history. There were two abortive attempts to create a lasting central banking system. Alexander Hamilton was the founding spirit of the First Bank of the United States, which survived from 1791 to 1811. Then in 1816, the Second Bank of the United States was established. It too was allowed to lapse in 1836. Its demise followed the Panic of 1837.

Panic describes the situation very well. Until the FED was established, the nation fell victim to a series of acute and severe economic dislocations known as money panics. The underlying reasons for panics were many and complex, but the results were all the same and obvious. There was not enough money to go around.

Typically, banks were pressed by heavy demands for currency. Since the supply of money was inelastic, institutions that had to have cash called in loans from their customers, creating a panic psychology.

Depositors reacted as was expected by withdrawing funds and in the process creating additional stress for the banks. All this had a rippling effect that led to widespread panics and failures of many banks that were basically quite sound.

There were other problems, too. Like a bewildering array of notes issued by banks as money, the fluctuating value of bank notes, epidemics of counterfeiting—just like today—and the lack of central supervision over the whole banking system.

When was the FED Created?

After still another economic crisis of major proportions, the panic of 1907, the nation had just about enough. Congress responded in 1908 by forming a National Monetary Commission whose recommendations led to legislation known as the Federal Reserve Act.

Signed into law by President Woodrow Wilson on December 23, 1913, the act was designed to provide for the establishment of Federal Reserve Banks to furnish an elastic currency, to afford means of re-discounting commercial paper, to establish more effective supervision of banking in the US, and for other purposes as well.

Ultimately then panic had led to order and the creation of an agency serving as the central bank of the US. The agency has since unofficially come to be known as the FED. Its responsibility in brief is to act as the nation's money manager.

The Structure of the FED—the Board of Governors:

The FED is a unique organization. The Chairman and Vice Chairman lead the Board. They are appointed by the US President and confirmed by the Senate. The nominees to these very important posts must already be members of the Board.

The terms for these positions are four years, but the Chairman and Vice Chairman may be reappointed for additional four-year terms as long as their term as Board Member is active.

The FED's Board of Governors is located in Washington, D.C. The FED is a unique blend of public and private interests—more private than public in many ways—that promotes the national monetary welfare of the US.

At the heart of the FED is the Board of Governors. The Board is composed of seven members also appointed by the President and confirmed by the Senate. Appointments are for four years, with one member's term expiring every two years.

These long terms were mandated by Congress in an attempt to remove the Board of Governors from political pressure and to enable the Governors to act independently and in the best interests of all the general public. For this reason, the FED is termed a quasi-governmental and/or independent government agency.

The Board determines general operating policies for the system as a whole, and formulated its rules and regulations necessary to carry out the stated purposed of the Federal Reserve Act. Its principle duties consist of exerting a sometimes strong, and sometimes not so strong, influence over credit conditions. They also supervise the Federal Reserve Bank and member banks.

The Federal Reserve Banks:

To assure that the FED would be attuned to the unique needs and differences apparent in a nation that spanned 3000 miles and linked together fishing villages in New England and Indian

Reservations in the West, Congress instituted a regional system of banks.

On the same day, November 6, 1914, the twelve Federal Reserve Banks were opened for business. The banks with their branches are:

1. Boston, MA
2. New York and Buffalo, NY
3. Philadelphia, PA
4. Cleveland and Cincinnati, OH, Pittsburg, PA
5. Richmond, VA, Baltimore, MD, Charlotte, NC
6. Birmingham, AL, Atlanta, GA, Jacksonville, FL, Nashville, TN, New Orleans, LA
7. Chicago, IL, Detroit, MI
8. St. Louis, MO, Little Rock, AR, Louisville, KY, Memphis, TN
9. Minneapolis, MN, Helena, MT
10. Kansas City, KS, Denver, CO, Oklahoma City, OK, Omaha, NE
11. Dallas, TX, El Paso, TX, Houston, TX, San Antonio, TX
12. San Francisco, CA, Los Angeles, CA, Portland, OR, Salt Lake City, UT, Seattle, WA

Federal Advisory Council:
Acting in an advisory capacity, this council confers with the Board of Governors on general business conditions and makes recommendations concerning matters within the jurisdiction of the FED. The twelve-member council is made up of one member from each of the Federal Reserve District Banks.

Each member is drawn from the commercial banking community and is appointed for a term of one year. The Federal Advisory Council meets in Washington, D.C. at least four times annually, and more often if called into special sessions by the Board of Governors.

Member Banks:
Directly and indirectly, the FED serves all of the nation's approximately 14,000 commercial banks. Probably less than that after this current financial economic meltdown of the past several years. Of this estimated number of banks, about 6,000 or roughly 40% belong to the FED.

FED members, however, account for about 78% of the total deposits held by the nation's commercial banks. Moreover, they have approximately 18,000 offices—although many of the nation's major banks have closed many of their branches during the past several years—or over 60% of all commercial banking offices in the US.

Who belongs to the FED? By constitutional law, all national banks are required to be members. State chartered banks—ones that were established under less restrictive State bank guidelines—that qualify with the more stringent Federal bank requirements may be admitted and granted membership on their request.

What the FED Does:
The FED functions as the nation's money manager by providing such essential services as:

a) Supplying coin and currency. Federal Reserve notes make up about 99% of the paper money in general circulation in the US. There is about seventy-five billion in coin and currency now in circulation (estimated). When a bank needs money, it orders it from the FED. In addition, the FED removes worn or damaged coin and currency from circulation.

b) Check processing. System-wide the FED processes approximately ten billion checks annually, representing about five trillion dollars.

c) Fiscal agent of the US Government. The FED maintains the largest checking account in the world—that of the US Government. All checks drawn on the Treasury are ultimately paid at the Federal Reserve Bank.

d) Marketing of government securities. When the US Treasury needs to borrow money to pay for the government's operations, the FED sells government securities such as Treasury Bills of 90 days to one year, Treasury Notes of one year of sever years, or Treasury Bonds of one year to seven years. Its services government securities by issuing, replacing, and redeeming these.

e) Control of US credit. The FED sets margin requirements for the purchasing of securities to prevent the misuse of credit. In cooperation with other agencies, it shares in enforcing truth-in-lending laws designed to protect consumers.

f) Loans. Member banks have the option of borrowing funds from the FED when necessary.

Federal Open Market Committee (FOMC):
The FED deals with monetary policy through its Federal Open Market Committee (FOMC), which consists of the seven members of the Board of Governors and the presidents of five reserve banks.

The president of the Federal Reserve Bank of New York is a permanent member of the FOMC, while the other four presidents are selected on a rotating basis. All twelve presidents, however, attend the sessions of the FOMC. Each month, the FOMC sets the guidelines for the volume of credit and money to serve the US.

The committee's monetary policy decisions are based on the economic intelligence reports assembled by the Board and the twelve Federal Reserve Banks. Monetary policy is designed to achieve full employment, whenever possible, economic growth, stable prices, within reason, as well as a satisfactory balance of payments.

Non-voting Reserve Bank presidents attend the meetings of the Committee, participate in discussions, and contribute information about economic conditions in their individual districts.

The purpose of the FOMC is to determine the nation's monetary policy. They hold eight regularly scheduled meetings each year in Washington, D.C. At these meetings they review economic and financial conditions and set US monetary policy.

The term monetary policy refers to the actions taken by a central bank, such as the Federal Reserve Bank, to help encourage as healthy an economy as possible. The actions taken influence the availability and cost of money and credit, which affect a whole range of economic variables, including output, employment, prices of goods and services, and just about everything else in the economy.

At each of its meetings, the FOMC decides whether or not to change its target for the Federal funds rate and, if so, how much. They also issue a statement after each meeting, explaining their decision. And these statements contain some important information about the FOMC's evaluation of the economy.

Monetary Policy—The FED's Number One Job:
The FED is charged with carrying out all of the mentioned duties, as well as some others. But the responsibility of determining monetary policy is its most crucial and vital service to the nation.

Basically, monetary policy is determining the right supply of money and credit the nation needs to stay as economically healthy as possible.

If there is too little money and credit, the economy may slow down too much and we may fall into a recession. Too much of these items, on the other hand, and there is a danger that the economy may overheat and we could suffer serious inflation.

Reserves, Discount Rate, and the Open Market:
How does the FOMC affect the money supply? Its primary tools are:

1) Bank reserves
2) Discount rate
3) Open market operations

Each member bank is required by law to set aside a certain percentage of its customer deposits as reserves. These banks must keep reserves as the district Federal Reserve Bank or as cash in their own cash vaults.

By increasing or decreasing the level of reserves in the banking system, the Federal Reserve makes it harder or easier for banks to make loans and/or buy securities.

So, for instance, if the FED lowers reserve requirements, it frees up additional funds in the banking system that can be used to make additional loans. And vice versa. This discount rate is the interest rate that member banks pay when they borrow from Reserve Banks.

A higher discount rate tends to discourage borrowing and, therefore, has a tendency to restrict economic activity. A lower rate makes it more attractive to borrow.

Of all the tools the FED has to influence economic activity, it most frequently relies on open market operations. To lower bank reserves, and therefore tighten the money supply, the FED sells government securities.

Since buyers pay for securities by giving the FED checks drawn on commercial banks, the immediate result is to draw down on the bank's reserves and restrict lending activity.

To do the opposite, the FED buys government securities and issues its checks to sellers who deposit them in commercial banks and thereby increase reserves in the banking system. The banks then have more funds available for lending and the money supply is expanded.

Who Pays the Cost of the FED?

Federal Reserve Banks generate their own income from two main sources:

1) The first and major source is interest from government securities, which are purchased and held by the Federal Reserve System to influence the volume of bank reserves in the nation. In 2008, the FED earned approximately five billion dollars from its government portfolio.

2) The second source of income is interest charged on loans granted to member banks. This earned the FED an estimated $15,000,000 (fifteen million dollars) in 2008.

Any earnings in excess of expenses are transferred to the US Treasury in Washington, D.C. Generally, the cost of running the FED has required about 9% of its earnings, dividends to member banks have totaled about 1%, and the remaining 90% has been paid back to the Treasury. In 2008, the FED from its earnings paid the Treasury about 4.3 billion dollars.

The Federal Reserve Bank of San Francisco has approximately 2,000 employees at its head office and its branches in Los Angeles, CA, Portland, OR, Salt Lake City, UT, and Seattle, WA. If you live in Alaska, Arizona, California, Island of Guam, Hawaii, Idaho, Nevada, Oregon, Utah, or Washington State, then you live in the 12th District territory of the Federal Reserve Bank of San Francisco.

What are some of the main responsibilities of the Federal Reserve System?

The FED's responsibilities include:

a) Conducting the nation's monetary policy to maintain employment, keep prices stable, and to keep interest rates relatively low.

b) Supervising and regulating banking institutions to make sure they are safe places for people to keep their hard-earned money and to protect consumers' credit rights.

c) Providing financial services to depository institutions, the US Government, and foreign banks, including playing a major role in clearing checks, processing electronic payments, and distributing coin and paper money to the nation's many banks, credit unions, savings and loans, and savings banks.

The FED also performs the following:

a) Conducts research on the US and regional economies.

b) Distributes information about the economy through publications, speeches, educational seminars, and internet sites, etc.

What are Interest Rates and Why are they so Important?
Interest rates are the price people pay to borrow money, or are paid to lend money. Interest rates, like other prices, are determined by the forces of supply and demand. Higher interest rates provide incentives for people to save more and to borrow less. Likewise, lower interest rates provide incentives for people to borrow more and to save less.

When interest rates rise, businesses are likely to invest less capital, and households are likely to spend less on housing, cars, and other major purchases. Lower interest rates are likely to cause businesses to invest more in capital expenditures and households to buy more big-ticket items.

In this way, interest rates affect the level of economic activity in the economy. The FED is able to affect the level of interest rates through its important monetary policy.

What is Inflation?
Inflation means that the general level of the prices of goods and services is increasing. When inflation is rapid, the prices of

goods and services that consumers are able to purchase goes down. In other words, the purchasing power of money has declined.

With inflation, a dollar buys less and less over time. It is not necessarily a bad thing, as long as it is kept in check and doesn't get out of hand. The FOMC tries to keep inflation low and stable in the long run because that helps the economy to keep growing over long periods of time.

When inflation is low and stable, businesses and households alike can make better spending and investment plans because they do not have to worry about high inflation decreasing the purchasing power of their money.

Example of inflation: If you are a young person and each Saturday afternoon you work for a neighbor for four hours and earn $3.50 an hour, you will earn $14.00 total each Saturday. Each Sunday afternoon, you go to the movies with your friends.

With your $14.00 you buy one movie ticket for $10.00, one popcorn for $2.00 and a coke for $2.00. Now over time, the price of movie tickets and food rises and eventually you spend the same $14.00 as follows: One movie ticket for $11.50, one popcorn for $2.50. (No coke).

This is a very simple example of inflation showing the prices of things bought at the movies has risen. The purchasing power of your $14.00, the total number of ticket and food items you can buy with that same $14.00 has declined. Now the same $14.00 buys you even less.

United Stated Annual Federal Statement of Revenue and Expenses

The US Government fiscal year begins on October 1 and ends on September 30 each year. Revenues consist of the following income items:

1. Individual income taxes.

2. Social insurance taxes. This includes direct taxes and payroll taxes from individuals and employers for disability insurance, social security, and other Federal retirement programs, hospital insurance taxes, and unemployment insurance taxes.

3. Use fees. This represents receipts of Federal department agencies, netted from gross outlays in Treasury reports, such as proprietary receipts from the public, receipts from off-budget Federal entities, and total undistributed offsetting receipts.

4. Death taxes. Repealed effective January 1, 2010 b y Public Law #107-16 signed by then President, George W. Bush, on June, 2001.

Expenses consist of the following items:

1. Social spending. Includes art, education, labor, health and human services, low income and public housing,

WIC, welfare block grants, food stamps, and other agricultural programs, and referral retirement programs, including the Social Security Administration.

2. Administrative agencies. Includes the SBA, GSA, DOE, GAO, Commerce, CPB, District of Columbia, EEOC, Export-Import Bank, FCC, FDIC, FEMA, FTC, Government Printing Office, Justice, Library of Congress, national Archives, and other independent agencies.

3. Emergency funding. Reflects outlays for anti-terrorism initiatives, disaster relief, bio-terror response, border security, inter-governmental joint investigation and prosecution, and air transportation security.

4. State and Foreign Affairs. Includes outlays for Department of State, Peace Corps, OPIC, AID, foreign military sales, and other international assistance programs.

5. Environment and interior. Includes EPA, National Park Service, Fish and Wildlife Service, Bureau of Land Management, Forest Service, National Oceanic and Atmospheric Administration, and major environmental programs of federal agencies.

6. Social Security Administration. Includes social security outlays for retirees and their relatives.

Banking in Russia:

Banking is a highly regulated business, with the government requiring all banks to meet a wide range of mandatory legislative requirements and to comply with a large amount of instructions and regulations coming down from the Central Bank of Russia.

Modern Russians, of course, inherited a banking system from the former Soviet Union, a fact that continues to affect the financial service sector, and was a primary contributor to a severe economic crisis in 1998.

In March of 1991, the Central Bank did establish procedures for the issuance of securities by commercial banks, and Russian banks also gained outlet to the stock market. Around that time, much of the State bank's currency exchange was auctioned off, with ten commercial banks and one other financial institution taking part.

After fifteen years of reforms, however, Russia is now home to over 1,100 financial institutions with a combined total of more than 3,000 regional banks.

The Central Bank of the Russian Federation—the Bank of Russia, headquartered in Moscow, is the country's central bank. Its functions are dictated by special federal law to include the exclusive issuance of ruble bank notes and coins.

Its primary responsibility if to protect currency stability. The bank recently launched a project designed to improve supervision of the banking system and encourage prudential reporting through the introduction of international financial reporting standards (IFRS).

Much of this project was designed to ensure credible accounting and reporting by the banks and financial institutions.

The new regulations also raised requirements for the content, amount, periodicity of the publication of financial information, and introduced accounting and reporting policies that now match international standards of good practice (GAAP). The same practices and accounting rules are used in the US.

As is the case with any central bank, the Bank of Russia is the main regulator of the banking industry. And it is responsible for the issuance of all banking licenses, as well as the setting of rules for banking operations and accounting standards. The bank is also a 'banker's bank', serving as a lender of last resort.

Overall, the Russian banking system has transformed from the centralized system of the Soviet era to the standard two-tier system comprised of central and commercial banks seen in most market-based economies.

At the core of the country's current commercial banking system are a set of large viable banks that have attained significant financial credibility.

Experts predict that these banks are highly likely to remain in operation under almost any foreseeable economic developments affecting the country as a whole, such as another economic dip or a currency crisis.

The three main banks, all formerly State controlled, that form the foundation of today's Russian banking industry, are the Agroprombank, subsequently renamed Rosselbank, the Promstroybank, and the Zhilstotsbank, reorganized into the Mosbusinessbank.

At the time of the 1991 restructuring, these banks were reorganized into joint-stock companies and became independent commercial operators.

All of this being said, the extent and quality of services offered by Russian banks are still highly rudimentary compared to what customer could find in any other European nation.

Russian banks, for example, are unable to offer highly diverse or even efficient customer services due to the continuing lack of sophisticated infrastructure across numerous sectors key to financial services operations.

Particularly lacking are the high-speed telecommunications and well-trained staff on which Western financial institutions are reliant. The largest and most established of the Russian banks do offer debit cards and varying degrees of direct or automated deposit and withdrawal systems. Some banks offer credit cards, but only to customers with impeccable and demonstrable credit ratings.

As a result of this lack of modernity in the banking system, cash transactions still dominate the day-to-day life—a situation many experts believe has significantly slowed Russian commerce in the 21st Century.

The Bank of Russia itself lists its primary goals and objectives as follows:

a. Increasing the protection of interests of depositors and other creditors of the nation's banks.

b. Enhancing the effectiveness of the banking sector's activity in accumulating household and enterprise sector funds and transforming them into loans and investments.

c. Preventing the use of credit institutions in dishonest commercial practices and illegal activities, especially the financing of terrorism and money laundering.

d. Promoting the development of the competitive environment and ensuring the transparency of credit institutions.

e. Building up investor, creditor, and depositor confidence in the banking sector.

A small Russian securities market has developed alongside developments in the rest of the financial sector and, although insurance services have had a historically negligent presence, the small but growing number of insurance companies that exist today are gaining a foothold and are slowly but surely working thought the nation's protracted period of financial reform.

It is widely believed and highly likely that as the role of the private sector in the national economy expands and the country develops even greater needs for sophisticated regulations and infrastructure, the Russian securities market and the role of various types of non-bank financial institutions will achieve concomitant growth.

Eight Largest Russian Banks

1. Absolut Bank
2. Bank of Moscow
3. Gazprombank
4. Promsvyazbank
5. Rosbank
6. Sberbank
7. VTB Bank
8. Alfa-Banking Group

Chapter Six
You Can Take That to the Bank

WHEN YOU FEEL very certain about the probability or outcome of a situation, based on your intuition and/or suspicions, some people are inclined to say something like: "This or that is going to occur, transpire, and come to pass, and *you can take that to the bank!"*

This is an old saying, and I want you to know I just love old sayings—I truly do. And I hope the reason is not because I am getting old. I do feel very certain that I am going to locate the culprit who embezzled the seventy-five million dollars from the IBBC bank.

And I am also certain that I will retrieve some, if not all, of the money for the stockholders and depositors of the bank.

I, Charlie O'Brien states here and now for the record that I will catch the thief and recover some of the missing millions—*and you can take that to the bank!*

I feel certain that I am zeroing in on a perp and they are most likely a lifelong paper pusher and career bean counter. There is always an audit trail, no matter how hard they try to cover their tracks.

It is like a telltale signature of the criminal. They'll break a protocol, an important correct procedure, and a red flag goes up. Deleted computer information is not really completely removed, as most people assume it is. It is still on the hard drive somewhere, possible on the internet which is everywhere, you know.

Then you have new spy software with information gathering at the main frame at the office computer system's department.

While I was in my temporary IBBC bank office in San Diego, I was contemplating my next investigative step or move to 'catch my thief.' Another old saying, of course.

I think I must have dozed off, and boy is that scary! I never used to do that. I must be getting 'over the hill,' as they say.

I received a rushed and pressing call from Howard Wallace, Deputy Director of the CIA via a scrambled voice radio circuit cell phone.

If you recall, I had assisted him with the CIA on the up close and personal Chernobyl Nuclear Power Plant visit in Pripyat, Ukraine formerly Russia and the Soviet Union.

He stated on the call, "Charlie, the DOD (Department of Defense) and the White House and NSA (National Space Agency) all need a non-US Government person to verify the launch of a supposed commercial satellite. It's being lifted off in Kazakhstan, also part of Russia, the former Soviet Union, at their Baikonur Cosmodrome Space Center."

A European EU 5 telecommunications satellite was going to be launched into orbit. It was valued conservatively at about two hundred fifty million dollars ($250,000,000), a quarter of a billion dollars to manufacture.

My job was to verify that indeed the launch takes place, and to safeguard US technology as best I could, and to help protect the US production company's assets and licenses. Northrup-Gruman, or one of the other biggies, had built the GPS satellite, or maybe it was TRW, I can't remember at the moment.

There would be people from the spacecraft manufacturer, the satellite telecommunications company, the satellite owner and billionaire Warren Buffet of the US, an important launch service provider, the US, Kazakhstan, Russian, Turkish, and British government monitors, representatives from the IAEA (International Atomic Energy Agency), Russian support personnel, and a whole lot of Kazakhstan military forces.

I would not have to worry about establishing security checkpoints, conducting security sweeps, or escorting non-US personnel while in US controlled areas around the launch pad. All I needed to do was to verify the launch goes off successfully, we hoped.

And I needed to make sure the Russians did not sneak another non-authorized military satellite onto the rocket booster as they have been known to do now that they cannot financially afford to send up a lot of their own rockets any longer.

I would also observe and report any suspicious activity around the launch area, and also notice if any representatives from Iran, North Korea, Venezuela, Cuba, Syria, or any other US hating countries around the world were attending the launch.

Howard said, "Closed circuit television systems (CCTV), vapor detection, fire and life-safety alarms, and temperature-humidity controls would all be monitored by a top-flight private security company from Sweden."

He added, "All of their very competent outstanding staff have US-DOD clearance and have passed the National Industrial Security Program training, which prescribes requirements, restrictions, and safeguards for preventing unauthorized disclosure of classified or confidential satellite information."

"Most of the company's staff are also instructed in International Traffic in arms regulations, espionage awareness, and technology safeguarding agreements between the US and the countries where these launches take place,"

Howard went on, "Prior to each different launch, the security experts receive extensive mission specific training and expert compliance training provided by the customer. The customer in this case is the very wealthy Warren Buffet, Chairman and CEO of Berkshire Hathaway Corporation."

And he said, "These people are highly trained security professionals. They have been all over the world several times, France, French Guiana, China, Germany, Japan, Kazakhstan (several times), Iran and Iraq. Access control is a major part of their job. Even after several assignment, they say the most exciting part of their job is watching the rocket take off."

I thought, hats off to them. I told Howard at the CIA, "I am right smack dab in the middle of an important IBBC bank embezzlement case investigation.

And now I might have to go back to Russia for a few weeks to one month? Normally, I would take on the satellite launch request with no problem and drop everything else I have going on if I could."

He replied, "Charlie, it's a matter of national security for the US. The US President is very concerned about all the satellites being launched around the world, with pay-load contents of who knows what. Possibly military hardware, spy links, missile defense systems, laser death rays, you name it."

How was I supposed to say no to Howard at the CIA? And to my President?

On some occasions in a man's life he has to cowboy up, as the old Western slang goes. Anyway, I would get some big bucks for this quick job, and all expenses paid by good old Uncle Sam (CIA) and a free trip to Kazakhstan, someplace I have never been before. Plus, I would make some brownie points with some VIP's in Washington, D.C.

So, I said to Howard, with a galvanized spirit, "You can count old Charlie in."

It appears that the diamonds and the IBBC bank case would have to wait a short time—maybe a week or so.

Howard told me before we finished our conversation that he did not like Russia. And his assistant, the Director of European Operations for the CIA, Abby Palmer, feels it is "ugly, inhospitable, with polluted air, filled with people speaking an incomprehensible language and fighting like rats for the bare necessities of life."

She believed that after the collapse of Communism, the population was still living in the shadow of the absolute dictatorship. It is an oppressive tyranny from which humanity and pure common sense has long ago been squeezed out, if indeed there had ever been any of these things in Russia. A more depressing place she could not imagine.

I guess she said how she really felt. She tells it like it is, and doesn't hold anything back about the former Soviet Union.

On my trip to Kazakhstan, I changed planes at the Lenin National Soviet Airport in Moscow—Mockba or Moskva, Russia. The big AC380 Airbus is the largest jet liner in the world, and too big to land at their smaller Kazakhstan airport.

I checked into my three-star hotel, the Tverskaya Hotel, because they didn't have any five-star hotels in town. So, I would be roughing it at a three-star, poor me. I was in the city of Baikonur, which is the closest city to the Cosmodrome Space Center.

How was I supposed to say no to Howard at the CIA? And to my President? On some occasions in a man's life he has to cowboy up, as the old Western slang goes.

Anyway, I would get some big bucks for this quick job, and all expenses paid by good old Uncle Sam (CIA) and a free trip to Kazakhstan, someplace I have never been before. Plus, I would make some brownie points with some VIP's in Washington, D.C.

So, I said to Howard, with a galvanized spirit, "You can count old Charlie in."

It appears that the diamonds and the IBBC bank case would have to wait a short time—maybe a week or so.

Howard told me before we finished our conversation that he did not like Russia. And his assistant, the Director of European Operations for the CIA, Abby Palmer, feels it is "ugly, inhospitable, with polluted air, filled with people speaking an incomprehensible language and fighting like rates for the bare necessities of life."

She believed that after the collapse of Communism, the population was still living in the shadow of the absolute dictatorship. It is an oppressive tyranny from which humanity and pure common sense has long ago been squeezed out, if indeed there had ever been any of these things in Russia. A more depressing place she could not imagine.

I guess she said how she really felt. She tells it like it is, and doesn't hold anything back about the former Soviet Union.

On my trip to Kazakhstan, I changed planes at the Lenin National Soviet Airport in Moscow—Mockba or Moskva, Russia. The big AC380 Airbus is the largest jet liner in the world, and too big to land at their smaller Kazakhstan airport.

I checked into my three-star hotel, the Tverskaya Hotel, because they didn't have any five-star hotels in town. So, I would be roughing it at a three-star, poor me. I was in the city of Baikonur, which is the closest city to the Cosmodrome Space Center.

When I went into the bank to get some foreign currency, I learned that a ruble is equal to a US dollar and that a 'kopyejki' represents a US penny. One thousand rubles is 'tysyacha rubly'.

Of course, you realize that an American dollar is actually worth more than a Russian ruble, a whole lot more.

I also learned that nomyer means number, and dyenji represents the term money. As I left the bank I said to the teller, "Spasibo bol shoye," or thank you very much. And she replied, "Pozhalujsta," or you're welcome.

Georgi and I wandered around prior to the launch, taking in all of the space center facilities the Russians had built before the wall came tumbling down. Now it's a big money maker for the Kazakhstanis. They let countries, as well as large private companies, use their beautiful facilities for a large fee, of course.

Prior to the launch, I used my trained PI eyes to see if there were any large Russian transportation vehicles or trucks carrying anything suspicious up to the spacecraft's launch pad.

I didn't notice anything obvious, but I would check the private security company's very detailed and comprehensive CCTV later, just to be sure I didn't miss anything.

Also, there did not seem to be any unauthorized representatives from any foreign countries wandering about. And there did not seem to be any suspicious activity going down, with one small exception.

A man named Boris Hopeyka, as I noticed on his name badge ID when he walked close to me on one occasion, a Russian, seemed to be following me everywhere I went. I could easily tell, with all of my surveillance training with the LAPD, that he was not watching Georgi. It was me he was after, for some unknown reason, which I was sure I would soon find out.

I wondered if it was just my imagination, but thought no I was being tailed alright. Was he FSB or Soviet military, Russian police, or just a bad apple that I would have to deal with sooner or later?

He very clearly was not an authorized visitor, nor an anxious spectator here to watch the out of this world satellite launch. His security badge, with a microchip processor, let him in everywhere than Georgi and I had been.

My new Russian pal and I apparently had the same sort of top-secret security clearance. I know that Georgi had done a lot of consulting work with the IAEA. He was also quite involved in the Russian space program, and served as advisor to the Russian military. I learned all of this from talking with him, pumping him for information.

Georgi lived in Moscow, not far from the splendidly beautiful St. Basil's Cathedral located near Red Square. My new buddy said to me, "Charlie, you should have been born a Russian. You would fit right in. You have a good eye, you are intelligent, and very inquisitive, and you get along well with people,"

I told him, "Spaseeba" (thank you), and added, "You should have been born an American!" Then, we both laughed a good belly laugh.

I excused myself from my pal and placed an encrypted protocol message to Howard Wallace at the CIA. When he decoded it later on, it would give him an update on my location and the status of my assignment.

It would also alert him to Mr. Boris Hopeyka, the smooth Russian who has been tailing me. I told Howard that if something were to happen to me, he should look at Boris first thing.

I recalled some things Howard said when we last spoke. Sending the encrypted message to him brought some things back to mind. He told me, "The Russians have little money and they want more of it. They want the good life that the rest of the West has. And, they want it now."

Howard had also said, "The Russians say, 'You Americans sit in your prosperous paradise with stables of cars and supermarkets full of inexpensive food, and think the unwashed hordes in China, India, and the Middle East are your enemies.

Not so. Your enemy is your largest economic rival, Europe, which has a larger economy than the US, in fact, it is the largest economy on earth."

He went on, "The Russians tell us that Europe has slashed taxes, jettisoned massive over-regulation, kissed socialism goodbye, embraced capitalism, and adopted one currency, the Euro. Europe is on the road to becoming a Federal State. Europe is the next super-power, not Russia."

Then Howard added, "An academic economist I met at a Washington, D.C. cocktail party told me that Russia will never be able to accumulate capital as rapidly as Europe and the US. The place is just too large, with a very harsh climate, and relatively few people to produce."

And, "The Russians will always pay more for the infrastructure on which a modern economy rest. Roads, factories, bridges, food, electrical grids, pipelines, and all kinds of distribution systems—everything costs more. Always has been the case in

Russia and always will be. The problem with capitalism is that it is just a game that good old Mother Russia cannot win."

Howard also said, "Europe is Russia's enemy as well. It has always been a natural enemy and always will be. Russia's foreign policy since the Middle Ages has been designed to protect itself from the European powers."

"As long as Europe was divided, and could be played off against one another, Russia with its vast space and lots of natural resources and poor population, had a chance. Now, with Europe united Russia's future looks grim indeed."

Howard continued, "Russia today directs most of their intelligence money and efforts against Europe, *not* America. With the collapse of communism, Europe has directed their spy agencies to provide an edge for their industrial efforts."

He went on, "Think of the A-380 Airbus made in Europe EC, the largest jet in the world. It is a completely different game these days. Without the ideological bogeyman to frighten people, they can more easily convince themselves that betrayal of their company is the same thing as betrayal of their country."

All of a sudden, as I reflected on these comments and opinions that Howard had expressed, I walked out along the perimeter of the satellite launch pad facility. I seemed to feel an uneasiness come over me. Nothing specific, though. It was just a bad feeling I had. Nothing I could put my finger on directly.

I felt it first. And then I heard it. Voila, another sniper shot? Not again! Luckily, I had leaned over to take a rock out of my favorite expensive black wing tip shoes, so the bullet just barely grazed my right arm.

It reminded me of the shot in San Diego some time ago. Déjà vu is here again. As soon as I cleared the cobwebs out of my head, I immediately wondered if the gift, the bullet, was courtesy of Mr. Boris Hopeyka, my Russian tailgater who was following me for some unknown reason.

I went to the first aid station at the security company's temporary office. They were very helpful and did a nice job of patch work on the wound. They asked if there was anything else, they could do for me.

I said that I would appreciate it very much if they would put a camera, a high-powered CCTV, on old Boris. Just in case he stayed around to finish the job.

I could not figure out who in the world would want me dead, way out here in the boonies. I must be missing something. I had not noticed anything out of the ordinary at the satellite launch site. Maybe I had missed something that someone else thought I had seen? Think big, I thought, real big!

What is going on here? The world was going to hell in a hand basket, as some people like to say. All these years of hard work, achievement, blood, sweat, and tears to boot, and it comes down to this? Being assassinated in a foreign country whose name I can barely pronounce? I can hardly wait to get back to the good old USA.

The satellite launch was spectacular, breathtaking, visceral, and unbelievable—all rolled up into one. Just absolutely majestic and almost spiritual as the heavens opened up to receive its newest visitor.

I had been to *Cape Kennedy* in the US, formerly Cape Canaveral, to see a space shuttle blast off in the 1980's, and I had always planned to go back again for years, but I have not made it back I am sorry to report.

I recalled reading about the famous Hubble Telescope. This launch today had stirred up my memory. Since its 1990 launch, the Hubble has been maintained and upgraded through five servicing missions.

Its last and final servicing mission was completed in 2009. I saw a gorgeous photo of Ant Nebula, the glowing remains of a dying sun-like star which gives us an early glimpse of what the future death of our own sun may look like some day.

Another photo from the Hubble showed a firestorm of a star birth in a nearby galaxy which contains some 200 brilliant blue stars and is 100 times the size of Orion Nebula in our own Milky Way. The last photo I remember seeing was of Jupiter's recent new red spot that suggests major climate changes on that planet.

The Hubble Telescope is named after the wonderful astronomer whose discovery in 1929 was that the farther a galaxy is from earth, the faster it appears to move away. This idea formed the basis of the Big Bang Theory.

The Hubble completes one rotation around the earth every 97 minutes. That's about five miles per second. In a car going that speed you could travel across the US in 10 minutes.

The telescope is the type known as a Cass grain reflector, and it captures its images by making use of the light bouncing off its primary and secondary mirrors. The lighter it collects, the better its vision.

Yes, as I thought about all of this and observed the satellite launch, I saw that it had gone off without a hitch. The Kazakhstanis really knew how to throw a party.

But I noticed a large Russian military truck leaving the launch site that I had not noticed before. It seemed to be in a hurry and it looked empty because it was bouncing a lot.

I wondered what had been in the truck before. I would have to investigate that more thoroughly, and watch me behind at the same time.

I looked up my old Russian pal again, Georgi, the scientist. He said, "Dobro pozhalovat" (hello). And I replied, "Spasibo bol shoye" (thank you very much).

Then he added, "Pozhalujsta" (you are very welcome). I think I am getting the hang of this Russian language stuff, although I still feel tongue tied when I speak it.

I did not tell my friend that I had just been shot. He could not see the bandage under my coat. It was very cold, as usual. It was always cold and rainy in the former Soviet Union. I don't know how many people can even live here.

I guess in the past few years since the iron curtain came down, a lot of people from the former Soviet Union, or Russia in particular, have moved to the US. There is a very large population of Russians in LA, and also in New York City, NY.

Unfortunately, from what I hear from law enforcement, they brought the Russian mob along with them. They are said to be more vicious and tough than either the Italian or Irish mobs.

I still was not sure whether George Valadimirnorov was FSB or Russian military intelligence. Until I found out, I did not want to tell him too much.

I just wanted to learn all I could from him about what was going on at the Baikonur Cosmodrome Center. But I would have to develop a plan to get him to expose which side of the ocean he was playing for.

I decided the best way to find out if Georgi was owned by the FSB was to tell him something that was declassified by the CIA but still appeared to be top secret. So, I contacted Howard at the CIA and got some information I needed in order to spring my little trap on Georgi.

I told him I heard a rumor that some of the Czar's Crown Jewels located in the Kremlin Museum had been switched with very good look-alike replacements and that the real ones had been sold off by some senior staff officers of the FSB.

If he was with them as part of the organization, he would contact them ASAP to pass on the information I gave him, not knowing that it was possibly totally unfounded and not factual. After all, he was no neophyte to the Russian Soviet Union rumor mill and secrets.

He looked very surprised when I dropped the bomb on him. He said, after calming himself down, "When some people get a lot of money, they do not care where it has been or where it comes from, just as long as it spends."

When I checked with my usual sources, I determined that Georgi had not contacted the FSB. He would have if he were on their payroll and if he truly were an agent operating for them and being paid to pretend to befriend me and follow me around Cosmodrome Space Center.

I could tell he was very upset and disappointed, but felt that if this were true that the senior FSB officers should handle their own dirty laundry or problems in house, so to speak.

And it appeared to me that he was not too happy with some of the things the gun-toting agency had done to some of his friends and countrymen in the past.

After confirming that Georgi was not the enemy (FSB), I was relieved and somewhat happy. I like him and I was glad he was not the one who had tried to kill me.

Now back to Boris. I thought how willing some people are to volunteer for unknown risks or to murder someone in cold blood when they are broke, hungry, very hungry, and sleeping on the cold hard ground. In Russia, this was one of the very few jobs where a man or woman could make serious money by being a hit person.

Most of the populous were so terribly poor that they didn't stop to think, however, that 'dead people never get a chance to spend their money, and this is an inarguable fact of life.'

The security company sent an officer to find me and give me a heads up. Mr. Boris was located in the waiting room in the site's comfortable control complex. They also gave me the description and license number of his SUV, a Lada model.

I located his SUV in the very large parking lot for the center, and I checked it out. I was able to get it open with a brand new, state-of-the-art door pick. Hidden in the back seat, I found a Russian made sniper automatic rifle.

Obviously, Boris was the guilty party who had tried to blow my head off. Granted it was not one of the best or most handsome heads around, however, I have grown fond of it and would like to keep it for a while longer.

Now all I needed to do was to determine why he wanted me DOA, dead on arrival. Besides the money that was on my head, of course.

I knew that he would be armed to the teeth and ready for anything, so I used a little ploy. I had the security company get him to come to their main office.
He had to leave all of his weapons in his hotel and his SUV because he knew they had metal detectors in the offices. No doubt he had noticed those before while checking things out.

Boris was obviously not a warm nor fuzzy person. He probably was difficult even on the day he was born—and on most days since then. But in the main office, I was easily able to handcuff him, with the help of the security officers.

He spoke in very broken English, just like my broken Russian. I needed to study more from my *Russian for Dummies* book, it was pretty obvious. He decided to spill the beans when I told him that I would not press charges for the attempted murder on myself, an American in a foreign country.

Boris was just a pawn in this chess game, and there was no reason I could think of to send him to a very desolate, bare necessities, terribly depressing Kazakhstan prison. I had heard the prisons were just as bad as those in Mother Russia.

Boris told me he was hired by a Russian military intelligence officer who had discovered that the CIA had sent me to observe the satellite launch. They had gotten permission from a Kazakhstan unethical space center official.

He allowed the Russian military to sneak a brand new very lightweight and state-of-the-art spy satellite onto the rocket just launched, for a very hefty amount in US dollars, not rubles of course.

I thought to myself that this is what had been loaded on the Russian military truck I saw making tracks from the site earlier. I said to myself out loud when alone again, "Now it's time for the gloves to come off, Charlie."

I immediately called Howard at the CIA in Langley, Virginia, over a secure encrypted phone line. I informed him of the Russian spy satellite, probably in the earth's orbit as we spoke.

I felt as if I were halfway across a dark abyss walking on a tightrope. But at the same time, I was finally starting to put all of the pieces together in proper order. And it felt good—really good.

The Russian military intelligence operative was not associated with the FSB in this situation. He hired Boris the hit man to take me to an early grave.

His name was Vladimir Plescovitch and he held a very senior position and had an office in the Kremlin building in Moskva (Moscow), right in the famous Red Square.

He was the officer in charge of the spy satellite program that had just taken place in Kazakhstan at the Baikonur Cosmodrome Space Center.

Howard at the CIA was able, due to his Senior Deputy Director authority, to send a special ops Army Rangers team to Vladimir's dacha (home) on the outskirts of town in a very nice secluded area.

Before you could say, "Mr. Gorbachev, tear down this wall," Vladimir was on a plane to a US military detention center somewhere in Poland.

They had wanted him sent to Gitmo prison, Guantanamo, Cuba, however the center was being considered for closure, due to unrelenting and ferocious pressure from the rest of the world. So, they were not accepting new inmates.

My Russian friend may very well have preferred Gitmo, as he knew he would receive very fair treatment and care there. Better than at the Polish facility. I was told that the Pol's and the Russian military were not especially fond of each other.

Soon the Russians would be hotter than a wet hen, but there was little they could do about it because theirs was an illegal international operation Vladimir was running for the Russian government.

I was only too happy to once again hop on a jet plane, an A-380 Airbus, of course, for my eleven-hour flight back to LA. I left

Kazakhstan with a short ride to Moskva (Moscow) on a T-134 Russian airliner, then went on to Heathrow International Airport in London before heading out over the Atlantic for my beloved Southern California in the good old USA.

Now I could get back to my IBBC bank embezzlement case after the short, but certainly not uneventful, trip to the Baikonur *Cosmodrome* Space Center.

While I was in Russia, and since it is not a frequent stop on my travel itinerary, I decided to call Anatoliy Krustalyov. He was an ex-KGB senior intelligence officer and a good friend of mine and my pals' Alexander (Alex) Smirnov.

Anatoliy is Georgian. Not the one in the US. He lived most of his life in Russia. He is now the Honorary Counsel of the Republic of Georgia.

He was so glad to hear from me, Charlie the PI. After catching up on things, hearing about his family, he told me an interesting story. Truth is sometimes stranger than fiction, and usually much more interesting.

Back in 1991, just a few months after the failed coup attempt in Moscow, Russia, a large commercial fueling gas station company FPG Corporation, was the first US company to do business in the former Soviet Union bloc nation of Georgia. Georgia broke away to separate from the Soviet Union in December 1991.

Shortly after that, the FPG from Southern California, opened the first western style location in the capital city of Tbilisi and established the Georgian Oil Company (GOC). This company is now owned by my friend, Anatoliy and some wealthy Georgian investors.

His brother, Dyengi Khrustalyov lives in California and started the FPG Company with just a few thousand dollars that he had saved, plus a little money from his friends and family, including Anatoliy.

He said that the business culture is still quite different in Georgia for a number of reasons. It was occupied for seventy years under the failed economic system of communism.

The fairly new nation (1991) was invaded by the Russian military in the summer of 2008 and much of their infrastructure was destroyed during the very short war, The Russian army was far superior to and much larger than that of Georgia.

The Georgian government expected the West to provide weapons and soldiers to help them fight the Russians, however, no one wanted to upset the Russians in what was perceived to be an internal matter. The Russians said afterward that they had 'spanked the little child, Georgia."

The position of Honorary Counsel is the highest diplomatic honor that a foreign government can bestow on a Russian or a foreign-born citizen. Anatoliy was born in Russia, but both of his parents were Georgian and born in the old country.

He said, “Georgia has been a beacon for emerging democracies in Europe, however, they made some mistakes that caused political conflicts resulting in business unrest that you do not find in the US.”

Finally, he stated, “In Georgia a particular festive annual occasion gathering is the Supra where many toasts are made and much wine shared. The celebration of Supra is always a great joy.”

Chapter Seven

Criminals Live Like They Are Never Going to Die

IF YOU READ the newspaper, which not many people do these days, or if you watch the news on TV or the internet, or on your hand held mini-computer phone device, or if you listen to the news on the radio in your car, bus, or plane, you can't help but notice that most *criminals live like they are never going to die.*

I am not sure why this is exactly. I should ask a criminal psychiatrist or a police psychologist for some insight into this unusual phenomenon.

Crooks just do not seem to worry about tomorrow like you or I, nor about getting caught for their evil actions. Nor do they worry about the pain they are causing their victims and families. Nor do they worry about their own families, for that matter.

The past just seems to push them continually forward in a never-ending career of crime and violence. They seem to me to have nerves of steel and ice water for blood. Like Charles (Charlie) Manson and his totally nutty 'family.'

PI's like me seem to live like we *are* going to die, and possibly soon. The very nature of our dangerous and volatile profession dictates that we must be ready to die at any given moment in time. Just like men and women in the military and law enforcement.

We cannot dwell on this fact, or it would drive us crazy or lead us to commit suicide, as a lot of PI's and police officers have done in the past. Some are forced to find a different vocation from the one thing they truly love and feel called to perform.

Like the dancers say, "I'm going to bring it and leave it all on the dance floor!" We detectives and PI's can say the same thing. But every once in a while, detectives or PI's have to leave their blood and/or their lives on the floor, unfortunately. This saying is sort of the PI's code of honor.

The phrase, "Live like you are dying", means to me to live with a singular and vital purpose. It also suggests that you should fulfill your own personal 'bucket list', or the list of things you want to do before you 'kick the bucket'.

By the way, the movie *Bucket List* with crazy Jack Nicholson and the great actor, Morgan Freeman, is very funny if you have not seen it.

I try to live with that kind of a very warm or hot passion in my life and my profession as a private detective. I don't always succeed, of course, but I do try my best.

I am only going to live once here on planet earth anyway and won't be back again. I work diligently to live as if I were dying in my professional life, family life, and my personal life.

As I mentioned earlier in my story, I have been shot several times. Not bragging or anything like that. 'Just the facts mam.' And any one of these times could have easily ended my life. Just so you know, I do not fear dying at all. I really do not.

There is an old saying, "We should walk the walk, not just talk the talk." And I believe that to 'live like you are dying' equals living your life passionately.

If you are going to live, then live! No halfway measures, no lukewarm actions. Live your existence with all of your heart, never lukewarm of halfhearted, nor unconvincingly.

I got a discreet call on my cell phone from an anonymous source who said she was not authorized to speak to me and she would not give her name. She was very obviously afraid of getting into trouble and/or getting fired if it got out that she had called me. I don't know where she got my number, but I was glad she called.

She said, "You should take a look at the bank officer named Thomas *Tommy* Frankhoffer."

She meant this in regards to my investigation into the seventy-five-million-dollar embezzlement at the IBBC bank.

As it turns out, *Tommy*, also nicknamed *Tommy Gun or Tommy*

Boy, and a few other names, was just as fast to fire employees as was his brother. Maybe even faster, some say.

He was the first Vice President at the San Diego regional office of the main bank, and just so happened to be the older brother of Carlos, *The Jackal*, Frankhoffer, the Executive VP and Board member of the

Corporate Board of Directors downtown LA. Carlos was the bank executive who assigned this present investigation to me a few weeks ago.

I heard that Tommy was real smart. When he was in 'sales mode' he was as smooth as a well-aged bottle of red wine.

And this guy could supposedly sell bank services to wealthy corporate executives whether they needed them or not. Also, he could talk his way out of prison, or sell stock in the Golden Gate Bridge in San Francisco!

I thought to myself, "Charlie, if Tommy is involved in this major theft, is his brother Carlos guilty as well?"

There I go talking to myself again. I think I should see a counselor and figure out why I am doing this all of a sudden.

Anyway, after some quick research I learned that Tommy had always been jealous of his brother Carlos. They had been very competitive throughout their entire lives.

I learned that Tommy, 51 and his very young and beautiful girlfriend, 25, spent a great deal of time at his expensive condominium, worth about two million dollars, located in Ensenada, Mexico, right next to the famous Donald Trump seaside Rosarito World Wide Resort and Casino.

It is right on the exquisite Pacific Ocean, just south of Tijuana, Mexico, and just north of the lovely and beautiful resort area and city of Los Cabos, in Baja California, Mexico.

And, it appears that Tommy has a large and expensive drug habit. Allegedly, he used pot (marijuana, Jamaica Red), LSD, prescription pain killers like so many of our famous Rock n' Roll stars use, uppers, methamphetamines, and other narcotics.

His girlfriend was said to only indulge in 'grass' and only once in a while. She was supposedly a nice young girl and people wondered what she saw in Tommy. Maybe it was the jet-setting, bling, glitz, and glamour.

His condition, if it were true, along with his brotherly jealousy, very well may give him good motive for an involvement with the reported theft. Not to mention, the motive of good old-fashioned greed. Like we see in the recent movie, *Wall Street.*

Tommy had the opportunity to move the money since he is a key executive in the San Diego regional office.

And he was readily able to trade on his brother's important and well-known name and position as Executive Vice President of the whole IBBC bank.

It would appear at first blush that Tommy lives like he is never going to die, nor get caught for that matter, if he is indeed guilty.

I called my PI friend, Carrie, in La Jolla. My Christian detective friends. I asked her to really dig into all of Tommy's financial records, credit bureau status, real estate holdings, and especially his bank accounts.

I asked Carrie to also check his girlfriend's background and bank accounts to see if he was hiding money there.

Carrie said it might take a while, but that she would get back to me ASAP. I knew she would get the confidential information very quickly, as she always does. The girlfriend's name, I told her, was Oriantha Green.

While waiting to hear back, I decided to return to my temporary office on the 20th Floor of the IBBC bank in downtown San Diego, overlooking the gorgeous ocean, the famous pier, and the lovely boat and yacht harbor. And, the beautiful Coronado Island, one of my all-time favorite vacation spots in the whole world.

When I got to my office, I made some calls and spoke with several disgruntled co-workers concerning Mr. Thomas Frankhoffer.

I had to promise immunity to them, on behalf of my good friend at the LA City District Attorney's office. I was able to arrange that favor quickly through a text message. This immunity was essential in order to get these people to spill the beans on good old Tommy.

The first employee I spoke with said, "I heard Tommy talking on the phone, saying something about diamonds being better than having cash or even gold.

Cash would be too hard to hide from the authorities and you usually have to pay a high fee each time you transfer it. Plus, it fluctuates in value a lot lately in these un-treaded financial markets."

He went on, "And, while gold is pretty and shiny to look at, it is way too heavy to move from one location to another without an armored transfer truck. And, you would need to explain to someone where you got seventy-five million dollars in gold, particularly with today's scrutiny."

The employee heard Tommy say, "Diamonds are much lighter than gold in weight and you can find a ready market to sell them at Jewelry Marts, diamond brokers, big vacation ships that sell a lot of jewelry to tourists, especially diamonds, and to several vacation spots around the world."

"And Tommy Boy added, 'Diamonds are forever.' Then, he laughed loudly to whoever he was talking to on the phone."

Another co-worker said, "I overheard Tommy on the phone right around the time of the reported theft, ordering two tickets for a plane to Moscow, Russia. One for himself and one for his pretty girlfriend. He said it was for a short vacation and while in Russia he had a little business to take care of involving jewelry and diamonds."

"He supposedly also made reservations for a five-star hotel in Moscow. Apparently, whenever Tommy travels, he goes first class, and he usually puts the cost of his many trips or vacations on the IBBC bank expense account, even if it is not connected with bank business in any fashion whatsoever."

Very interesting, I thought, to myself, and actually said it out loud, interesting indeed.

The third employee said, "I overheard Tommy telling someone on the phone he has detailed plans and once they come to fruition he will retire and live like a king in Baja and travel the world whenever he wants."

After learning this very valuable insider information about Tommy Boy, I was pretty certain he was as guilty as sin, but I needed more proof. I hoped my friend Carrie the PI would provide the key information, especially about his bank accounts.

And, I needed to determine if his brother, Carlos *The Jackal*, was involved with him, making them both white collar criminals. Or was Carlos just a very mean spirited, arrogant, and narcissistic man?

I have always felt that Carlos was JDLR (just doesn't look right). There is just something about him. You know what I mean?

Carrie called me first thing in the morning and woke me from a night full of nightmares. Several involved my unfaithful, selfish former spouse. She got the information I needed, as I knew she would, of course.

Financial Records: Tommy's assets totaled approximately seven million dollars. His liabilities were about six million, leaving him with an adjusted net worth of about one million dollars. Most of his equity was in very questionable assets.

Credit Bureau Status: From three major bureaus, Equifax, Experian, and TransUnion. His credit score was fairly high due to his good long-term employment with the bank, however, on closer notice he had several credit cards and most of them were maxed out.

And some were delinquent as well. And his real estate mortgage payments were behind. The banks were getting ready to foreclose on all three of his properties.

Real Estate Holdings: County property records showed he owns a condominium in Ensenada appraised for about two million dollars, and a large estate and ranch on the outskirts of San Diego worth about two and a half million dollars. Not bad, however, he owes the bank about four million five hundred thousand dollars on his subprime mortgages.

Bank Accounts: It turns out Tommy Boy has multiple bank accounts. It appears he floats money back and forth to cover his checks. His main account is at IBBC bank, and is used mostly as a depository for his salary of five hundred thousand dollars a year.

He has an account at Bank of America and Citibank in San Diego, Barclay's Bank, London, Grand Cayman Bank, Cayman Islands, and Wells Fargo Bank right next to **IBBC** bank in LA on Bunker Hill financial district. And of all things he has a numbered Swiss bank account in Lucerne, Switzerland. Surprise, Surprise!

If you add up all of the financial information, it is very evident that Tommy is bankrupt. He has just not yet filed the necessary paperwork with the US Bankruptcy Court.

Somehow, Carrie also found out that Tommy owed money to about half the bookies in San Diego and Ensenada. A great deal of money, too, she was told. Boy, she is good. Besides his drug and alcohol difficulties, it turns out he also has a big gambling problem.

Just like John Gotti, the former mob boss from one of the largest crime families in New York City, Tommy bets on almost anything.

Judging from this information, as well as what I had developed from the bank employees, Tommy Boy really badly needed the money that he allegedly embezzled from his bank employer. He was in debt up to his eyeballs and he could never pay it back. Not in this lifetime anyway.

After finally gathering all the evidence and proof I needed to be 100% absolutely sure that Thomas *Tommy Boy* Frankhoffer was the perp in the seventy-five-million-dollar embezzlement of customer funds, now I needed to talk to Tommy and get answers to several hard questions I had for him.

I knew he would not be glad to see me at all, and that I was going to totally ruin his day and rain on his parade.

When I asked his boss, IBBC bank San Diego Regional President, Mr. *Smitty* Smith, where Tommy Boy was, since he was not in his luxurious executive office, he stated that Thomas was on vacation in Mexico at his beautiful and exquisite condominium in Ensenada with his pretty young girlfriend, Oriantha Green.

Apparently, she used to be his secretary before she quit. That's how he knew her. When I checked with the bank's San Diego internal travel department manager, Gloria Gossett, she stated that she had indeed purchased two first class tickets for Tommy last week. I wondered if he had been tipped off that I was investigating him and checking on him very closely.

I also wondered if he had been behind the sniper who shot at me when I was walking on the lovely beach strand in San Diego while working on a case there with Carrie, PI. If he was the one who instigated my near demise, he would pay for it, and soon.

The travel agent added that the two tickets were not to Mexico, but to Moscow, Russia. If would seem he just told his staff and his boss that he was going to Ensenada so they would not become suspicious. Everyone knew that the couple went there

all the time, so it would not seem out of the ordinary or like he was trying to make a getaway.
Now I needed to go to Moscow, former Soviet Union, and fast, to confront Tommy Boy ASAP before he, the money, and the diamonds disappeared like a thief in the night.

I prayed that I would be able to a) find him, and b) recover some of the seventy-five million dollars in high grade brilliant cut proportioned diamonds.

When I got to Moscow, the first thing I did was to take a taxi to my favorite place to lay my head at night, Peter 1st Luxury Hotel. It was located just across the street from the Fabulous Red Square. It was a beautiful five-star hotel from back in the day in Moscow, Russia.

The hotel clerk said, "Dobroye utro (good morning) back to me. She must have understood me well enough even with my pronounced American accent. I took a couple pictures of the hotel just for the fun of it.

I told the nice Nadia Solvyev who spoke impeccable English, as well as six other languages, that I needed to rent a new Russian automobile for a few days. Possibly an Avtovaz sedan or a Lada sports car.

She took care of all the details and billed the IBBC bank, per my request. Then she recommended the Lada sports car. She assured me the model of car would make me feel young again!

I thought that was very sweet of her, however, it would take a lot more than a sports car to make this old PI feel young again!

I thanked her and said Dasvidaniya (goodbye). More Russian, aren't you impressed?

My suite was just amazing and it looked right out over Red Square with the exquisite St. Basil's Cathedral and the Kremlin in view. There was a complimentary basket of fresh fruit plus a bottle of Stolichnaya vodka on the beautiful old antique dining room table.

I ate the fruit right away. I was starved for some reason. It was tasty and wonderful. I passed on the Vodka, as I am still on the wagon. I will keep it though, and use it as a recycled birthday gift to one of my business associates who drink the hard stuff.

As soon as I could, after taking a long nap from my eleven-hour flight from LAX, I called my KGB friend Alexander (Alex) Smirnov. He was glad to hear from me again, and said how much he and his wife had enjoyed my last visit. I felt the same way, of course. I asked about his family, then asked about things in general in Russia.

He confided, "Under the Communists, Russian society was as closed as a locked bank vault, with half the population being paid to spy on the other half. In Russia today, there are countless numbers of people anxious to sell all sorts of technological information. You can buy bucketsful of secrets on Moscow street corners."

"Criminals and con artists are as busy as beavers. Since the FSB cannot plug all of the real leaks, they are also busy selling bogus secrets. Apparently, they create phony classified files to sell to the information hungry foreigners, including in the US, and this is the only growth industry in Russia."

After some reflection from his soul. Alex said to me, "All the lies the Communists told, the crimes they committed, the lives they shattered, the thousands of people they murdered, that was the foundation of the Soviet State. And the whole colossal sand castle fell of its own weight. They had no financial base."

"If that wasn't enough, then came the aftermath. The now anti-communist Nomenklatura, bureaucratic elite of the former Soviet Union, soldiered on as before, spouting propaganda about freedom and democracy."

"What a dreadful joke. Same people, different song. They stole the foreign aid money donated by the West, NATO, the US, and the rest. They looted the National Russian treasury, sold top military secrets and equipment, and literally robbed their own fellow citizens of everything they owned, just to line their own pockets.

They destroyed the worker's paradise of Stalin, Krrushchev, Andropov, Kosygin, Brezhnev, among many others, too many to mention."

"Civilization collapsed in Russia, as well as in the rest of the Soviet Union countries all over Europe. That was the optimists' take on it anyway. Cynics said it never really existed there.

Clearly, the liberal civilization of the West never existed in Soviet Russia, which had gone directly from a totalitarian society ruled by Czars, to one ruled by absolute dictators. Some trade off, right?"

"Now, with the dictators gone, no one rules except the FSB, formerly the good old KGB." Alex finished.
I said, "I think that will change, of course, as the Russians like dictatorship just like Americans love freedom and democracy.

They were comfortable only in an authoritarian, autocratic society where everyone behaved and did as they were supposed to do. And the people at the top set the standard. The Russians did not know how to live any other way, it is sad to say."

I told Alex, "I need to find someone here in Moscow. A man named Thomas Frankhoffer and his girlfriend. I think it might be like looking for a needle in a haystack, but if anyone can find him, I bet it will be you, Alex."

He was a premier intelligence professional if there ever was one. Also, he had great street cred in Moscow, as well as in most of Russia.

I picked up a tail at my hotel and he was probably FSB.

The FSB, successor to the KGB, had the same paranoid bunch running things, still doing all of the very nasty stuff, but now they say they are not communists anymore. As if that makes a whole lot of difference in an authoritarian society like Russia.

PROFESSOR ALAN DALE DICKINSON

I used a different passport on this trip to Russia. Not the US one I used last time. I used my Belgium Passport instead. I paid a lot of money for it and it is just as good as any. But the Russian Federal government must have picked me out somehow.

I knew it was not one of Viktor Kharchenko, *The Fisherman's*, men because he would be unaware that I was back in Russia.

I hoped I could keep it that way for as long as humanly possible. I really did. He will not be very happy with me, if and when he finds out that old Charlie the PI from America was now back in Russia.

I met Alex at a terrific restaurant, the Ukraina Café, which is close to Vladimir Lenin's Tomb and Red Square. I had made some moves after I left my hotel and I lost the FSB tail I had.

Alex and I laughed merrily as we chatted away. Me in my fractured, broken, and semi-intelligible Russian. He spoke impeccable Russian, of course, as well as very good English, French, German, Italian, Spanish, mandarin Chinese, and Farsi, among a few others!

While I am getting better at Russian, I am still not very fluent. Luckily for me, most people in Moscow speak passable English. I needed a lot more practice, I decided after our lunch. Also, lucky for me I have a good teacher in Alexander Smirnov.

We had borsht (beet soup), and the food was all so delightful that later on when we were leaving, I could barely walk when I got up from the table.

I thought, "Charlie, the PI, the little porker!" I am going to have to go back to the gym as soon as I get back to LA. I have eaten so much rich food during the past month, since the IBBC bank is so good about paying all of my food and travel expenses.

Somehow, Alex had already located Tommy Boy for me! He was staying at the majestic Maxima Slavia Hotel in Moscow. It was not that far from where I was staying, which was convenient. His girlfriend was staying with him, heaven only knows why!

And Alex had heard through the grapevine that Tommy Boy had picked up his precious seventy-five million dollars' worth of precious diamonds from *The Fisherman* (Viktor) and he was now looking for serious buyers both inside and outside of Russia.

Furthermore, he was not planning to return to the US ever again! Tommy Boy was somehow aware that I had discovered his embezzlement scheme and how he was on the lamb.

A momentary twinge of panic gripped me. For some unknown reason, I recalled what Viktor, *The Fisherman* had said, that if he ever saw me again, he would kill me with no questions asked!

I don't know why, but that thought popped into my head again. Being back in Moscow was kind of like playing Russian roulette.

I was walking on a tightrope without a net, and I very well knew it. If things were to go south for me, I could always call Howard, CIA, or one of my close contacts at Interpol, New Scotland Yard, MI-5 British Intelligence, or a few Congressmen I know well in California.
The Fisherman always has a lot of gun-toting squarish shaped men on his payroll who would shoot me just as fast as they could pull the trigger.

Viktor could take my return to Russia as his perceived view of my intrusion into his business to a whole new level. A level that would be way, way up there, if he really wanted to. And from what I have learned about him, he just loves to accelerate his game—game on!

Viktor also has sharpshooters who usually do not miss their intended targets, possibly me. His profit from the sale of the diamonds to Tommy was probably about thirty million dollars US, and that's not peanuts.

Even though *The Fisherman* was one of the richest men in Russia, and possibly in the world, it was not unusual behavior for him to kill someone, or take them out, for a lot less. A whole lot less. Let's say, just for a few US dollars.

Maybe he would not erase someone for a few rubles, dyeryevyannyj or 'wooden' worthless in Russian, but I would not bet that he would not. And I certainly would not want to take that chance. I guess that's why they pay me the big bucks.

I heard that *The Fisherman* smokes two or three packs of unfiltered Camel cigarettes a day. I didn't know you could even buy this type of smokes anymore. My dad used to smoke those, and Pall Malls, back in the day.

Apparently, the greedy tobacco companies have found these cancer sticks are big sellers outside the US, mainly in Europe and China. Viktor supposedly taps them on his thumbnail to settle the tobacco, just like the cowboys did in the old Wild West.

It's not a nice thing to say, of course, but just to be brutally honest, it would not be terrible if Viktor were to become too ill from smoking to worry about this little PI.

Just to let you know, I have analyzed my current very precarious situation in this case I have put myself into. If *the Fisherman*, the FSB, or one of the other Russian intelligence or police agencies were to get hold of me, all the king's horses and all the king's men will never put old Charlie the PI back together again.

I said to myself, not out loud this time, "Charlie, good friend, this situation is about to get real exciting, really quick."

I came up with a brilliant plan. At least I thought it was a great idea. I had Alex and his close friend, Vitalyi Vronsky, also former KGB like Alex, pose as Russian FSB agents. They would detain Tommy Boy so he would stay at his beautiful hotel, the Maxima Slavia in Moscow in his large and very expensive suite.

Then I would come over and question him about the embezzlement and, of course, the seventy-five million US dollars in diamonds.

The next night, Alex and Vitalyi went to the Maxima Slavia Hotel with forged FSB official looking identification badges in letter holders like the CIA uses when they are not undercover, of course.

They also carried a phony notice on fancy FSB headquarters letterhead authorizing the hotel management to assist the two agents in any way possible. An 'or else' was implied somewhere in the fine print.

The hotel manager, Sergei Bazorov, was very cooperative as was to be expected. He was a very impressive type, as managers in expensive hotels usually are. He was intelligent, professional, and a tall, handsome man. A very Russian looking guy who dressed to the nines impeccably.

He wore an obviously very expensive imported Italian wool three-button suit. Two buttons would just not do here. With a beautiful pure silk tie and a matching pocket kerchief. He wore custom fitted black wing tip leather shoes, and suspenders in lieu of a belt.

The hotel manager was absolutely perfect for his role and was probably wearing three or four thousand US dollars, not rubles, worth of clothing and attire.

Alex always preferred American made fire power to the Russian made guns. He felt they were more dependable in a pinch and less likely to jam or misfire. Those things are kind of important when your life is on the line, as I am sure you can appreciate.

The only Russian made weapon that he likes and swears by is the AK-47, but not the Chinese made one. The Russian AK shoots and never seems to wear out.

The Chinese AK-47 is of poor quality and does not hold up well at all. He usually carries a Ruger MP 9mm submachine gun and a Colt 1911 A1 automatic .45 caliber pistol.

Alex knocked on the door to Tommy's suite and said in Russian, "Sir, room service you ordered."

As soon as Tommy Boy opened the door, Alex and Vitaliy pushed their way in and said they were FSB local Moscow city agents.

Luckily for his girlfriend, Oriantha Green, she was out shopping, probably for Russian mink coats, new dresses, and red high heel shoes.

Once Tommy Boy was convinced by my two friends that he was not getting out of the suite and couldn't call for help, he settled back in his big comfortable chair in the formal sitting room area.

He picked up a glass of very potent Stolichnaya vodka. He apparently didn't drink Smirnov vodka, or maybe they didn't even carry it in this posh five-star hotel. The bottle was half-full, as I like to say as an optimist. A pessimist would say half-empty.

That's when I came through the door into the suite, not a moment after my two phony FSB agents Alex and Vitaliy.

Tommy Boy looked me over very closely, just like he probably did when some customer wanted to borrow several million dollars from the IBBC bank. He also looked a bit nervous.

But not much. He's been around the block more than once and has been involved in some very stressful negotiations at the bank before.

Besides, he knew Viktor, *The Fisherman* didn't he! He was probably saying to himself, "What can these three people do to me with all my contacts here in Russia, in Novokuznetsk, Siberia, Mirna City Diamond Mine in northeast Russia, and the deadly *Fisherman*?"

Viktor was nobody to mess around with. Tommy Boy was right. He was a stone-cold merciless killer. People who knew him said he is a time bomb with a lit fuse, just waiting to explode.

Then after drinking a big shot of vodka, Tommy Boy said to me, "Soon I will be filthy rich, without a doubt richer than I ever dreamed."

"Maybe not as rich as Bill Gates, the Microsoft founder, or Steve Ballmer, Warren Buffet, Sumner Redstone, Carlos *Slim* Helu from Mexico City telecommunications, Ingvar Kampradin Sweden's Ikea owner, Lackshi Mittal in India steel mills."

"Or Sheldon Adelson in US casinos and hotels, Bernard Arnault in France's luxury goods and services, Amancio Ortega in Spain's clothing and apparel, Li Ka-Chink in Hong Kong, China, a diversified entrepreneur, or David Thomson of Canada with his inheritance and investments," he went on.

Tommy Boy added, "Actually, doing this embezzlement thing is fun, challenging, and very lucrative."

He went on, "I think I will buy an island close to Macaw, Hong Kong, China and live like a little emperor. I think Ensenada, Mexico is just a little too close to San Diego and the bank I stole from for my comfort level."

"And Mexico has been handing over people recently who are wanted for crimes in the US. In the good old days, the Federales police would let criminals stay in their beautiful country just as long as they had some dinero (money) to support themselves and make donations to the local law enforcement agencies."

"I will clearly miss my beloved Baja California. It is one of the most beautiful and picturesque places in the whole world. And

I should know. I have traveled extensively, on the IBBC bank's expense account, of course."

"Boy, my brother is going to be madder than a wet hen. And my whole family will be extremely upset with me. Oh well, that's the way things go sometimes," Tommy concluded.

Tommy Boy is narcissistic with delusions of grandeur. He's a legend in his own little mind, and obviously still a drug day tripper.

He added after a brief pause like he'd done some kind of soul searching, "What I have done, I have done. There is no going back now. I cannot wipe out a jot or a tittle of it even if I really wanted to. I am totally, completely, and absolutely 100% committed now."

His eyes were dark and brooding and very sinister as he spoke. Did Tommy Boy really think he could sell himself, his very soul, to the devil and then just walk away?

Once his precious diamond money is gone and he can sing 'that was the day the money died,' he would come to the realization that his greed had been at the center, the vortex of this whole mess.

I was totally into my PI mode now, after listening to Tommy Boy rattle on. My mind was on the case and it was just about to come to a big conclusion one way or another. And I thought, 'you can take that to the bank!'

I made Tommy Boy a proposition that I believed he could not refuse. Kind of like the mob used to say in the US years ago when they very strongly made an offer to someone for a transaction and to let that person know that it was very smart to accept their offer, rather than to risk the alternative of saying no.

Think baseball bats, pliers, chainsaws, and meat packing plants, not to mention incomplete cement bridges or foundations next to the late Jimmy Hoffa, the famous Union organizer.

I told him he could keep one third (33%) or approximately twenty-five million US dollars from the sale of the precious diamonds. Or I said he could keep his third in the form of diamonds, and I gathered this is what he would prefer, from what I had learned about him.

His part would be to return the two thirds (66%) worth of diamonds, or convert them to cash for a small extra fee and give the fifty million dollars back to the IBBC bank via myself.

As a bonus, I informed him that if he did this, he would not be extradited back to the US to stand trial for embezzling the seventy-five million dollars from his former employer, IBBC bank.

So, he would not have to face the certainty of a conviction and twenty-five years to life sentence. Since the bank was a national or federal one, and not just a state bank in California, he would face a much stiffer, much longer, sentence if convicted, of course.

But there was no chance he would not be convicted. You can 'take that to the bank.' And, I thought to myself that as part of the agreement, a very important part, he would have to give the names of anyone who had assisted him with his shady criminal scheme.

This included his beloved girlfriend, if she had been involved. I told him that he could still buy his exotic island off Macaw and live like an emperor with twenty-five million US dollars.

I thought out loud to Tommy Boy, "Anything you decide to do right now is all your responsibility." Then I thought to myself, "Charlie, you have been way too generous with your offer. You should have only offered him 25% or about eighteen million, seven hundred fifty thousand US dollars."

I clearly wanted to take credit for a job well done, and to have the IBBC bank happy with my work and settlement in retrieving the seventy-five million dollars. But after all, if I returned fifty million or two thirds (2/3) to them, it would be a whole lot better than nothing at all.

And, it would prevent the bank from having to make this whole mess public, which would be a disaster of the first order and magnitude.

They could probably bury a loss of twenty-five million dollars under losses on foreign currency exchanges or something like that, with the CPA's approval. Anderson and Anderson, the accountants, were one of the biggest firms in the US and very well respected.

Well it's history now, or as we say in America, I can't put the horse back in the barn now that I have let it out the door, so to speak.

Tommy Boy looked like he had just sucked on a grapefruit. He really seemed to believe in his little scheming heart that he had gotten away with his grand embezzlement plan and that he was going to be able to keep the whole nine yards of the seventy-five million dollars.

He stalled for a moment and drank some more vodka. The bottle was almost empty now. I could see the wheels spinning in his crooked head. He thought that a third would be better than nothing, zero.

But he would rather keep it all, the greedy son of a gun. If he could just put a bullet in my head with the 9mm pistol in his desk, and the report/recoil with his silencer would barely make an

audible sound. But alas, what about the two FSB agents? That was a major insurmountable obstacle for him.

After a seemingly very long period of time, Tommy Boy said to me, "What if you let me keep fifty percent (50%) or half, and I will kick back to you under the table a whole million dollars? No questions asked."

I did not take too long to respond. I said flatly and quickly so he would completely understand. "Thanks, but no thanks. That is not how old Charlie here does things."

He got out another bottle of Stolichnaya vodka from the bar, and asked if I wanted a splash. He didn't bother to ask Alex or Vitaliy if they wanted any. He was sure they would just say they were busy. I just passed.

My two friendly book ends pretend FSB agents just stood there not talking. They were looking very intimidating. Alex stood right by the suite door and Vitaliy was watching the window because it had an open balcony.

All of a sudden, two Russians came busting through the suite door! One square shaped man and a very athletic looking woman. Both looked like Ninjas, wearing black masks and black tight clothing.

They came through the door like speeding bullets. The man immediately went for Alex and the woman almost cart wheeled over to Vitaliy.

The intruders did not appear to have guns with them. And, they did not appear to need them! The man had Alex pinned to the floor in seconds and the woman had Vitaliy in a strangle hold.

It took me a moment to realize what just happened. Then I galvanized myself and quickly drew my .40 caliber Glock automatic pistol from my shoulder holster. About the same instant, I grabbed my lightweight .357 Smith and Wesson revolver from my ankle holster.

I shot the man with my Glock, since he would need the bigger bullet I surmised. Then I shot the woman with the .357. It was over in a heartbeat, a nanosecond, and they dropped like a bad habit.

All of a sudden, my left shoulder ached. I looked down and saw a Ninja star was stuck in it. Apparently, one of the visitors tossed it at me when they crashed through the door. I guess in all the adrenaline rush and excitement I had not felt the sharp thing. I sure felt it now though.

Tommy Boy never moved from the big chair, and he was not at all startled. Apparently, he had hired two body guards to follow and watch out for him, since he had control of seventy-five million US dollars' worth of diamonds.

The diamonds were not in the suite, of course. He was too crafty for that. For now, he had them hidden someplace safe.

He did not seem to feel bad about the two dead Ninjas. People like Tommy Boy do not feel things like normal people would. They just don't play by the civilized rules that dictate the way the rest of us play. He was the kind of guy you did not let out of the house to play with the nice kids on the block.

I felt very sorry to have had to shoot to kill the two invaders. It was killing or be killed. I knew that. And I had to save my two Russian friends, Alex and Vitaliy.

They were only there at my request. I crossed my fingers for the families of the two bodyguards and tried to put it out of my mind for a minute.

Tommy Boy decided to accept my very generous offer, as I suspected he would. He really didn't have much of a choice. A hefty prison sentence at Club Fed, or twenty-five million dollars. Pretty easy decision, wouldn't you say?

As part of his plea deal with me, he had to roll over on anyone else involved in any fashion whatsoever in the theft of all that green stuff.

He said, "My brother was not involved at all, no way. Neither was my girlfriend." I was kind of glad about the girl, but I don't know why.

He added, "I did have two accomplices though. Donn Lowely, Senior Vice President at the LA central cash vault of IBBC bank, and Frederick *Red* Abbott, Senior Vice President at the San Diego regional cash operations center."

I believed he was telling the truth, as he had no reason to twist the truth at this point.

The two individuals who helped in the embezzlement had seriously miscalculated. They played for all the marbles or bank notes, and underestimated that the authorities and/or police detectives, or a private investigator like myself, would eventually catch up with them.

They would be singing the song, 'the day the money died', very soon. They had forgotten about the ubiquitous detectives and private investigators, everywhere at once it seems. Apparently, they had each received one million dollars for their part in the IBBC bank embezzlement scheme.

I called my friend at the LAPD, the Deputy Chief Jim Bowen, and I told him to snag Donn Lowely at the bank's office building at 333 S. Hope Street, Bunker Hill, in LA, just to make sure he didn't jump on a jet plane when he heard about Tommy Boy rolling over on him.

After that, I called my contact at SDPD to arrest Red Abbott at the IBBC bank's San Diego regional office. I did not want him sneaking across the Mexican border. It's only a hop, skip, and a jump from where he works and lives.

Neither crook would have to serve hard time, unfortunately. They probably will just be sent to a Club Fed, a white-collar minimum-security prison. They would, however, have several years to reflect on their greed and also on what a good criminal and salesman Tommy Boy was.

He clearly was a cold, calculating and merciless excuse for a human being. It will be perfectly clear to them that he sold them down the river and left them there without a paddle.

I hated to let Tommy Boy leave Russia with all that cabbage ($) for his little island paradise off Macau, Hong Kong, China. But a deal's a deal.

Your word is your 'bond' when you are a PI. You don't have much else to work with on the street to obtain cooperation from contacts, confidential informants, or criminals.

I felt it was my responsibility though, to contact Howard Wallace at the CIA, a friend at *Interpol*, and another associate at *MI-5* in London to request that they have their local agents in the area Tommy Boy was headed to keep an eagle eye on him.

As soon as he did something stupid, as I am absolutely certain that he eventually will, then he will be picked up immediately and incarcerated in a very deep, dark, and damp prison in China.

I said Spasibo bol shoye (thank you very much) and added Dasvidaniya (goodbye) to my two good Russian friends, Alex and Vitaliy.

I paid them their fee, plus a little extra bonus in US dollars of course, because they had almost been killed while assisting me with the retrieval of the fifty million for the IBBC bank. I believed they earned every penny of it, and then some.

Just as I had previously felt when I was in Russia before, I could hardly wait to jump on a jet plane and head back to my beloved sunny Southern California in the good old USA.

I looked around and said *Dasvidaniya* (e.g. goodbye) to Mother Russia, thank God! And in a heartbeat, I was gone!

The end.

www.ingramcontent.com/pod-product-compliance
Lightning Source LLC
Chambersburg PA
CBHW030616310726
48979CB00003B/749

* 9 7 8 1 7 3 2 6 2 8 3 1 1 *